snow
BLACK

THE SEVEN RASTAS & OTHER SHORT STORIES

snow BLACK
THE SEVEN RASTAS & OTHER SHORT STORIES

TALISHA JOHNSON known professionally as Tee Cee is currently a Development Researcher and Presenter who has won eight BBC commissions for her ideas, including three series. At age 16 she became the self-published author of the first edition of her children's book 'Snow Black, the Seven Rastas' and Other Short Stories and was dubbed a 'Black History Month hero' by Birmingham primary schools.

Off camera, Tee Cee is a qualified Career / Life coach who can be found inspiring the next generation through professional speaking and empowering young women through a platform she founded called 'Not Your Average Girl' which supports young women in media, particularly TV and digital through positive personal and professional development.

snow
BLACK

THE SEVEN RASTAS & OTHER SHORT STORIES

Talisha 'Tee Cee' Johnson

Cover design & layout by David Springer 2019
Illustrations by Glory Alozie 2019

For the girl who never felt good enough. You matter.

THE SEVEN RASTAS & OTHER SHORT STORIES

CONTENTS

Colour me in

CLAIRE'S MYSTERY

Back at home

Silence drowned the entire atmosphere of the house. Faces were blank and voices didn't utter a word. It had been two weeks since their daughter Claire had died, and the reality of the whole situation still hadn't sunk in. The house had come to a complete standstill. It was a great shock that was clearly unexpected. Family and friends had gathered with cards and flowers, all on their way to place them at the crime scene where she was found. Grandma Wendy-May did her best to keep everything and everyone in order; it was the only thing she could do, well, to detract her attention from thinking about her beloved, precious granddaughter.

Simon, Claire's dad, sat with his head resting in the white disfigured shape of his unsettling palm. He was a tall, strapping fellow, a dark brunette with hazel eyes; hazel eyes that were now filled with sleepless nights, tears and sorrow. As for her mum, Yvonne, she had lost two stone and returned to that awful habit of smoking again, which Claire hated! Her skin was pale and lifeless, with eyes drooped like curtain rails and black mascara smeared across her eyelids. She looked like a twig on legs, with bones popping out of her chest; it was an awful sight to bear. Simon glared at the cigarette scornfully; he despised it just as much as his daughter did. Rising to his feet, he was quick but also extremely careful to take it out of Yvonne's quivering hand; he casually placed his arm around her shoulder.

"Everything will be okay, love," he whispered gently into her small, dainty ear. Her face rose for their eyes to meet and, bursting into a great flood of tears, she buried her head into his broad shoulder.

"I want Claire! I want my little girl back!" she screamed helplessly at the top of her lungs, drawing everyone's attention to her. Simon tried to hush her in a calm and collected manner.

"Don't touch me!" she scowled at him.

With a strong mighty force, she untangled herself from his grip, leaving him hurt and embarrassed, and ran out of the living room with her hands clasped over her pink face. A pink vulnerable face, drowned heavily in endless teardrops. She ran and ran: down the hallway, up the stairs, across the landing and then she stopped. Something had drawn her hasty actions to an immediate halt. Taking a deep breath and a step back, she had brought herself to take the first step into Claire's bedroom since she was taken.

She looked around the room. Everything was in its rightful place, jeans on the floor, tops flung over the sides of the wardrobe, dressing table full of hair and makeup products, an unmade bed full of clean (and dirty) underwear. Last but not least, Jimmy, Claire's *'I can't possibly live without you'* purple teddy bear, sat on Claire's pillow. It was given to her at the age of seven months and had never left her bedside. The 'perfect' bedroom she'd call it if she were there. Yes, everything just the way Claire liked it. Yvonne smiled gently, wiping a great mass of green mucus from her runny nose.

"She was just your typical, ordinary teenager," she said in a calmer, more relaxed, tone. Placing herself on the untidy bed, her hand reached for Jimmy. She ran her fingers through his fluffy, smooth purple fur, stroking it slowly. Her nose then rested in his head sniffing the very intense aroma of his being. As she did this, she rocked him gently at a rhythm-based pace.

It was in that particular quiet time, that time she had spent while in Claire's room alone, that she began to reminisce about the short life of her daughter. The life that was unfairly cut short with no explanation.

"Is there any justice in this world for a mother like me? Can anybody hear me up there? Is there anybody who even cares?" Yvonne questioned, and questioned life itself, until she reduced herself to more outrageous cries. She couldn't possibly contain it.

It just kept on coming and gushing out like a boisterous waterfall.

Her mind then began to wonder, wondering where and what Claire might be doing at this present moment in time. Was she happy wherever she was now? Was she sad? Was she being looked after by somebody else up there? A firm knock at the door alerted her attention instantly.

"I want to be left alone," she demanded in a monotonous tone, whilst coming out of her train of thoughts.

She heard a low toned, "Yvonne love, it's me, can I come in?"

Simon lowered his voice even more, and repeated the question. He sensed her hostility strongly and was more mindful this time around not to upset her again. As he finally took the hint that his wife wasn't going to respond or acknowledge his presence, he entered the room, at his own risk. He joined her where she was seated on Claire's bed. His attention was drawn straight to Jimmy, who was still laying in her arms.

"Jimmy," Simon chuckled, as if trying to engage in casual conversation.

He then pulled her close, kissing the side of her wet cheek. His grip was tight and firmly secure, as if to make sure that this time she didn't escape.

"Yvonne, I love you, and I promise that we will get through this together and I will do everything in my..."

His last words were choked underneath a gulp of breathlessness as his eyes began to water.

After a while, teary eyes turned into more sniffs and snuffles. Simon and Yvonne had been sat in Claire's bedroom for over an hour. Simon caught a glimpse of the time from Claire's *'every girl's* **gotta** *have one of these Betty Boop clocks'*, realised that time was passing and that they still needed to go and lay flowers where Claire's body was found. It was a two and a half hour journey as it was, and they were running incredibly behind.

"I think its time we got going, don't you think, love?"

Yvonne looked up gazing into his eyes for about four seconds, and then nodded in agreement.

In the forest

She'd lost them. A whole big group of people had suddenly vanished before her eyes. Why? She did not know and, how? She was certainly unsure. As she walked the dark ominous surroundings, she remained completely oblivious to the deserted destination in which she was. A look to her left, and up rose the black daunting vengeance of darkness, seizing her crystal green irises. A look to her right, it was as if ocular delusions of treacherous foul creatures blustered her brain. They gouged and snarled at her flesh as if it were some vivacious enterprise to eat. One look up, and the gloomy appearance of the barbaric skies frowned down at her with grim-visage faces. A look down, she felt the grimy mounds of earth sinking deeply into the shattered soles of her petite feet. One look forward: fear gripped her internal organs, tension had captured her body, as if she had been taken hostage. This was just the beginning. The beginning of Claire's mystery.

Voices. She heard voices. A whisper, whimpers, cries, laughs. Sounds. **Boom. Bang. BANG!** She heard sounds. People. Was it people she could hear?

No!

She felt like she was losing her mind, thinking she heard things that weren't even there.

"Hello, is anybody there... *anybody?*"

The awkwardness of silence taunted her. It made her exceedingly insignificant. It teased and tormented her. Mad. A series of various thoughts and emotions raced heavily, like flashes of burning lightning, through her troubled mind. She solemnly longed, craved and hoped that she was not alone.

There was something very mysterious about this forest. She contemplated to herself on its sense of surrealism.

"*Claaiirrree...Claaiirre*" something anonymously whispered in the distance.

"CLAIRE!"

What was that? She turned in swift motion scanning her atmosphere with curiosity. Was she hearing things? Or did she really hear her name being called?

In the car

"It's strange innit? Very strange. I guess you don't expect your children to die before you." Yvonne still hadn't reached the stage of acceptance.

10 minutes later...

"Nearly there love," Simon turned to his wife, gracing her with his warm embrace. It was as if he hadn't even heard her speak a moment ago. He then glanced back to the site of the road, accepting the fact that he was probably going to be ignored.

"Umm hum," She responded randomly after a short period of time whilst blowing her frizzy hair back with a tremendous huff. She fidgeted impatiently in the car seat whilst continuously biting her nails until they were right down to the pink soft flesh on her fingers. Simon removed a hand from the steering wheel and pulled Yvonne's hands away from her mouth.

"Aren't you scared, Simon?"

He looked at her briefly whilst trying to multi-task his focus on the road at the same time.

"What made you ask that?"

"I don't know, well I guess maybe... because I am."

Leaving one hand on the wheel, he reached for her hand and placed it to his heart.

"Can you feel this beating?"

"Yes. (*Pause*) Yes I can, *very fast* actually."

"That's how scared I am."

Her hand remained there for a while before finally withdrawing it. Nothing more was said. Supposedly, there was nothing more to be said, and on they drove the rest of the journey in complete silence.

Back in the forest

Her throat stung for the yearning of a drink to quench her crusted oesophagus. Reaching her hands nervously behind, fiddling for her rucksack, it was her great horror to find that it was no longer there. Vanished. Disappeared. Gone.

"My bag!"

At that, she panicked, becoming even more petrified. Her pace of walking became more active in motion.

"Somebody! Anybody?"

Claire wanted a way out; she was desperate and afraid. Speeding up even more, CRUNCH! Hesitating on her hands and knees: she had stumbled, a crunchy familiar substance seemed to have disintegrated before her eyes. Staring at it strangely, she picked It up examining its content carefully with great admiration.

"My, my bracelet?"

What on earth is it doing here? She wondered, and why was it so dirty and decrepit? Looking at it, she saw how its interior was slowly rotting away. *How strange! Wait a minute, what's going on?*

Suddenly, her eyes were drawn to another familiar object in the near distance. Getting back on her feet, she ran hastily over to where the object was visibly placed. She stopped herself immediately. On the ground was her rucksack, surrounded by red and white banners, cordons.

Cordons, why are there cordons surrounding my rucksack?

As she stood puzzled and extremely confused, she then began to notice more of her belongings scattered in the territorial area, and flowers.

Flowers?

My face! **Missing! What?**

Claire! **Dead?**

Is this some kind of practical joke? Claire became annoyed and frustrated at the sight of this.

"Why do they think I'm missing? Dead? I'm right here, lost...But fine. I don't understand!"

Tearing wildly through the banners, she grabbed hold of the newspaper article containing her face. In bold clear print it read...

"Claire Robinson, aged 15 died two weeks ago after going on a school camping trip. It was claimed that she had wandered off, losing the rest of the group that she had come with. Unfortunately, after this incident

she was not seen again, until her body was discovered shortly after, next to an endangered bush of thorns in the forest."

Claire dropped the article to the ground instantly, her eyes widened and she started breathing heavily.

WHAT huh! I huh, CAN'T huh, BE huh, DEAD huh!

Her mind couldn't function properly and her breathing became even heavier. Tears began streaming down her pale face as she couldn't bring herself to believe the truth.

In the car

"You have arrived at your destination," the sat-nav announced boldly. Simon looked over to his nervous wreck of a wife, as she froze timidly on the car seat.

"It's time, Yvonne."

"No, no, Simon, I can't do it, I really can't do this."

It was just too much, she was about to face the place where her only precious baby girl had lost her life.

"Yes you can," Simon reassured her, "we're in this together, are we not? I'm right here with you, don't be afraid." He managed to persuade her to get out of the car with a few words of comfort; he helped her along as she hid her face away in his chest. She was like a lost puppy that had gone astray. Family and friends also followed them closely behind ready to say *goodbye*.

The forest was dead and dreary, Yvonne loathed the sight of it as she visualised her daughter lost, alone and afraid.

"My poor baby! My poor baby! She must have been so scared."

The thought of her being alone in such a forsaken environment was unfathomable.

Back in the forest

Moments later...

Claire watched as family and friends appeared before her very eyes.

"DAD! MOM!" she cried helplessly.

It was a relief to her soul to see them finally coming to her rescue. She felt loved once more, as she could only assume that everybody had been looking for her all this time and now she was found.

They all began placing cards, more flowers and décor around the banners, whilst completely ignoring her presence. Claire found this rather strange. She then went closer to make sure that she could definitely be seen this time.

"DAD! MOM! LOOK IT'S ME!" She reached out her arms; strangely, as she went to hug them she passed straight through them. She observed her arms and hands, horrified by what had just happened. So it was true, she was dead. Loud cries echoed through the atmosphere as people mourned deeply for her loss.

Claire refused to give up easily; she couldn't quite come to terms with it all and refused to believe the truth.

"NOOOO!! I'M NOT DEAD! LOOK, I'M HERE. DAD! MOM! NAN! ZOE! JADEN! I'M HERE, LOOK, PLEASE LISTEN TO ME! WHY ARE YOU INGNORING ME? PLEASE, I'M HERE!"

Her loud cry for help, turned into an indescribable pain. Claire had *finally* realised it was no use because they couldn't hear her.

I guess this was just another mystery. However, not just any mystery. *Claire's mystery.*

Colour me in

tWISteD tUESDAY

The sunrise shone brightly through the double-glazed windows as she lazed untidily in her bed. Her legs were spread widely, at the edges, as spit dribbled like a running tap from the sides of her thin lips. How *'unladylike'*, her mother always grunted, whilst doing her daily routine of attempting to drag her typical teen out of bed each morning.

"Time for school, Missy, UP! NOW!" she always yelled, with her daughter's reply usually being just a *"SNOOOOOOOOOOOORE!"* well, that's if you can call that a reply. More like a hideous noise.

An hour later...

"AAAAAAAAAAHHHHHHHHHHHHHHHHHHHHHHHH!!"
The noise she usually made when she was late.

"What was I thinking? Too much TV last night, again."

She tumbled from the bed, flat on her face, landing in an awkward position on the bedroom floor with blue pillows and a cream duvet suffocating her entire face.

"I'M OK!" she shouted, as if trying to reassure herself.

Glaring wide-eyed at her alarm clock, she saw that it had gone off an hour ago. Rushing to her feet in a speedy flash with eyelids still half closed, she threw herself into the long mirror hanging perfectly on the wardrobe door. "OMGOOOOSH!" she screamed to the horrendous look of the monster on the other side. She then dashed for the bathroom, having the quickest shower of her life. When finally dressed in the ugliest epic school uniform of educational history, she encountered the mirror once more.

"Right, only one way to fix this madness, "WHERE IS MY MAKE UP BAG?!"

1. **Primer.**

2. **Eyebrows.**

3. **Slap on a bit of foundation.**

4. **Concealer...."ARGHhh, ran out, AGAIN!!"**

5. **"Never mind!" Blend, blend, blend.**

6. **Mascara.**

7. **"Where is my gloss?...Ah! There you are. DONE!"**

"There, better already, Jasmine Kelly is ready to go."

Plunging the skin beneath her eyes down, she tried to revamp the fat, lumpy white bags from under them. Finally, realising that she really had no more time for fanning around, she grabbed her Nike rucksack and headed down the stairs and out the front door.

Panting and puffing all over the place, she finally realised that skiving off P.E lessons for the last year wasn't the wisest of choices. As she stopped to catch her breath, the school bus came speeding past.

"WAAAAIIIIIIIIIIIIIIITTT!! NOO, STOP! STOP!" she yelled as she gasped for litres of oxygen. As she stopped running, she watched as the bus drove into the distance with familiar school faces staring, pointing and laughing out of the windows.

"ARRGGH! Just my luck, darn it!"

Time had passed, and dragged on terribly. Jasmine refused to even bother to show her face on school grounds, instead she felt her day would be better spent wallowing in her own self-pity. I mean why should she care? It's not as if she wasn't just missing out on, I don't know, six whole hours of valuable education or something silly like that. If she had spent more time sleeping than binge watching Netflix then she wouldn't be in this mess now, would she? She huffed, and puffed and blew a great steam of frustration out.

Whilst walking down a deserted street of silent traffic and practically no atmosphere, a small ginger cat approached her.

"EUGH, CAT! GOooo Awaaay!" she shrieked, whilst looking at it with a threatening body posture and wagging her fists in front of its face. Alarmed, the ginger cat ran off swiftly.

"Yeah, that's right you walk away and don't come back, and good riddance to you too! I mean what do I look like, a vet?"

10 minutes later....

The ginger fluff ball had returned.

"For goodness sake, leave me alone will ya, I could have you done for stalking you know."

This time instead of running away, the ginger cat stayed put.

"Shoo! Go away! Grrrrhhh! Psssstt!!"

t still stood in refusal to budge; she folded her arms at his stubbornness to do as he was told.

"Fine then, be disobedient for all I care."

After a while, she just possibly couldn't resist the velvet ginger fur and the black beady eyes; pure innocence, you could also call it.

"Ooh, who am I kidding, I suppose you're kinda cute, okay you can stay with me, I could do with the company anyway, just behave yourself erm... whatsyahface... Mr, that's it, I'll call you Mr!"

And on they both walked along the isolated pavement, side-by-side, hand in paw.

An irritating rattle hummed through Jasmine's ears, her view began to accelerate like a mammal with monocular vision. She couldn't quite distinguish where it was coming from. Suddenly looking down she saw Mr hitting an object with his paw. The content looked exquisitely ravishing, but very delicate. It was layered in fine metallic gold décor, with the interior embroidered with sky blue jewels.

"Wow, it's absolutely gorge! Good boy Mr."

Jasmine ran behind a closed corner; Mr followed, scurrying quickly behind. She didn't want anyone to see her new-found possession. She was highly fascinated as she shook it forcefully to see what it contained.

"AAAAAAAAAAAAAAAHHHHH!" she shrieked.

"BOOM. BANG. BAAMM. CAABAZZ!" was the noise of the mighty explosion that had been unleashed from the golden object.

Jasmine couldn't believe the hazel iris fragments of her eyeballs. Before her appeared an enormous blue creature, it's black hair tied up high into a perfect ponytail and it's blue arms dressed in the shiniest gold bracelets she had ever seen.

"M, m, m, Mr! Mr," she screamed.

Glancing behind, Mr was nowhere to be seen.

"WHO DARES TO AWAKEN THE QUARTERS OF THE ALMIGHTY GENIE?!"

Jasmine, not knowing what to do or say for herself, stared straight back into the genie's eyes with nothing but confusion eating away at her mind. The genie gazed at her with a gruesome look of disgust with his black, menacing eyes.

"Little girl, are you deaf? Did you not hear my question? I demand you to answer me at once!" he bellowed.

Sweat showered Jasmine's forehead.

"My, my, my name...Erm... I have a name...erm it...it...it's J...Ja...Jas... Jasmine." Stuttering like a warm blooded mammal that had just been dropped into the base of Antarctica, she couldn't seem to make sense of any word, phrase or sentence that left her mouth.

"I'm afraid I don't speak the language of 'Gibberish', although my father did suggest for me to take it for my GCSE's, but never mind about that. Now ...now where was I? Oh yes, I am growing sick and tired of amateurs like you, unleashing me from my, might I add, very comfortable lamp!"

Jasmine stood puzzled, having no idea what the genie was babbling on about.

"Now there, look, you see what I mean! The rudeness of you! Absolute cheek I tell you, if it were my way, I'd have your head! Now hurry up, make your three wishes, so I can pack up my book of tricks and be gone!" He folded his arms boldly while staring at Jasmine with one eyebrow raised towards the air.

"Now wait a minute Genie, well that's if you really are a genie, what on earth are you talking about? Wishes, tricks, what?"

A humungous purple vein emerged at the top of the genie's forehead.

"How dare you question if I'm a genie! Huh, am I a real genie? Of course I am a real genie, you dim-witted time waster of a human being! Now listen up good missy, cuz I'm only gonna say this once, and once only. Now here's the deal:

Number 1: Farse human unleashes Genie from lamp.

Number 2: Unfortunately Genie 'has' to grant farse human three wishes.

Number 3: Then farse human can get out of Genie's face and then Genie can, as they say, 'gwarn bout 'im business.' CAPEESH!"

The genie fumed so hard that steam was being released from his ears.

Jasmine pinched herself several times, just to make sure that she wasn't dreaming. Nope, turns out she was living in reality. Living it loud and clear! The genie grew impatient as he waited and waited for Jasmine. He dragged his thick blue eyelids down in front of his face with his broad blue fingertips, as if experiencing some form of traumatic breakdown.

Jasmine didn't know what to do, whether to take this blue stranger seriously? Could he even be trusted? Did she have anything to lose by trusting him? She then sighed heavily, finally giving in and reassuring herself that she had nothing to lose.

"Right Genie, I've decided I have nothing to lose by attempting to take your word for it, even if it does sound a bit bizarre, besides I have nothing better to do and three wishes doesn't sound that bad, I suppose. I could use a bit of fun to brighten this disastrous day anyway."

"Hmm, well then, I see you have finally smelt the hot chocolate and come to your senses, but just before you get all excited, *I must inform you that with ALL, and I repeat, with ALL three wishes you will receive a consequence.*"

"A consequence?" Jasmine questioned. "What do you mean a consequence? I'm sure Aladdin didn't have consequences with his wishes!"

"WELL MY DEAREST, I WOULD THEN ALSO LIKE TO POINT OUT THAT THIS ISN'T SOME POXY DISNEY MOVIE WITH CARTOON CHARACTERS, THIS IS REALITY BABY, SO GET WITH THE PROGRAMME EINSTEIN!"

Jasmine stood in a state of shock as the genie's every word echoed off the surface of her body, leaving her bewildered.

"Alright, alright, you don't have to shout you know, right *wish number one*, hmmm let's see, think carefully Jas, think wisely," she murmured to herself. Rubbing the smooth contours of her chin, she wondered, thinking long and hard about what to ask for; she wanted something that would benefit the whole world and not just herself. But what could she ask for?

"It is 2072, and Jasmine is still thinking!" The genie muttered sarcastically. Finally, a huge grin spread across Jasmine's face.

"I know, I've got it, get ready for this one Genie, I wish for 'WORLD PEACE'."

POOF!! And it was done.

It was like rush hour on Boxing Day except people were rushing to greet one another. Jasmine's hand had been shaken by so many different strangers it grew tired and sweaty. She was repulsed.

"Whoa, talk about 'Living together in perfect harmony!'"

She wasn't used to so much attention at one time, especially seeing as half the attention was from people she had never seen in her entire life. People wouldn't leave her alone, pulling, prodding and giving her huge bear hugs. It was of course a complete violation of her usual preferred personal space and boundaries.

"That's enough!" she yelled as she stampeded through a crowd and headed for the nearest retail shop. She found many electrical appliances to harbour behind, until she felt it was safe to leave. Facing ahead of her was a 30 inch plasma, flat screen TV.

"Wow!" Jasmine gasped in amazement. "My favourite Netflix shows would look even better on that." She moved closer to it sneakily, trying not to blow her cover; some politician was on there, giving another controversial speech... *Again!*

"Aye? What's this?" Jasmine had to check if her ears were deceiving her. "WHAT? NOO! They are not serious! They can't do this!"

The biggest most absurd crisis had occurred, and by the looks of things there was nothing Jasmine could do. The House of Parliament had just passed a new law stating children in the UK should attend school seven days a week for four hours a day instead of six. There were even interviews shown with parents all over the country agreeing to this decision. Everyone was agreeing with one another, even if decisions were as ridiculous as this one.

Jasmine had quite frankly had enough, and didn't even hesitate to un-wish such a delusional nightmare before things really did get out of hand.

"And 5, 4, 3, 2,1... BINGO! Oh back so soon Jas," the genie laughed hysterically with his bulging stomach flubbing up and down like a trampoline.

"That wasn't funny Genie," She hissed, pulling an evil look out of the corner of her eye. "And by the way it's Jasmine to you."

"Hey, hey, hey, I did warn you, so don't get all 'MISS DIVA FEISTY FABULOUS' with me honey." He waved and clicked his hands in the air imitating someone with a diva-ish attitude.

"Anyhow, swiftly moving on, time for your second wish, or do you need some recovery time from that dreadful last wish, hmm?" The genie was purposely winding Jasmine up, and she knew it.

"NO, I don't need 'recovery time', thank you. I am quite ready to make my second wish." She smiled at him smugly, trying not to be discouraged by his mocking.

Thinking long, hard and more carefully about what she was going to ask for this time, she decided on a second wish.

"SHUT MY MOUTH AND CALL ME 'THE' JASMINE KELLY, I'VE GOT IT! ... *'I WISH TO BE THE RICHEST PERSON IN THE WORLD!'"*

POOF!   And it was done.

Masses of money stacked in numerous piles surrounded her environment as she sat prestigiously on her royal throne.

"Yes, Miss Kelly."

"Right away, Miss Kelly."

"As you wish, Miss Kelly." Servants and butlers acted within an instant on her every wish and command. It was surreal. Incomprehensible to even believe. Diamonds, rubies and pearls were visible on every body part known to the human race.

"OMD! OMD! I have golden eyelashes! I have golden eyelashes! This is Crazy!" Yes 'tis true, she had the whole enchilada, and much more.

Her fingers had grown exhausted from all the clicking and snapping she had been doing for the last hour. To her advantage, she had been provided with a special cream from one of her butlers to relieve these aches in her fingertips. UNBELIEVEABLE. There was actually something for everything in her kingdom.

"I want!"

"I want!"

"I want!"

It just kept coming up, like word vomit. She wasn't about to let this once in a lifetime experience pass her by lightly, she was taking advantage of every opportunity she was given.

As she soaked up the tremendous new lifestyle that she was now living and breathing, an alarm sounded with a loud triumph. The atmosphere was no longer filled with glistening spot lights of antique chandeliers, but with red flashing warning lights along with the daunting repetition of the word 'INTRUDERS!'

The entire kingdom rushed around beneath her feet frantically.

"RING THE ALARM!"

"BOLT THE DOORS!"

"RUN FOR YOUR LIVES!"

"EVERY MAN FOR THEMSELVES!"

Anxious to know what on earth was going on, Jasmine Kelly demanded an explanation and she wanted one urgently.

"You there!" she hurled pointing her index finger directly towards a lost looking servant trying to find an escape route.

"Y-ye-yes your highness," he stuttered nervously as his hands hid deep inside his mouth.

"I demand you to give me an explanation for this chaos, FILTH, disruption to my kingdom!"

"The kingdom is under attack your majesty!"

Her eyebrow rose sharply towards the air, she grew impatient at this grumbling fool before her eyes stating the very obvious.

Sarcastically she replied, "You don't say," as if she didn't hear the irritating and loud repetition of 'INTRUDER!' like everybody else. She continued, "My question is WHY?" The servant began laughing hysterically.

"Something funny?!" she was not in the least amused.

"Your highness, your kingdom is under attack at approximately every 7 hours without fail. You're the richest person in the world, and everybody wants your money."

She sat back a moment, realising what she had bargained for. Genie did say my every wish had a consequence, she remembered.

"Will my life be like this forever servant....servant? Servant?" Looking around, the servant was no longer in her sight. It really was every man for themselves. She knew her life wasn't safe to live like this, and she didn't want to live it in fear for the rest of her days.

"No! Enough! Enough! I don't want to live the rest of my life in fear! No more! GENIE MAKE IT ALL STOP!"

"Oh back so soon," the genie laughed whilst manicuring his nails.

"It's not funny!"

The genie sarcastically held up his thumbs and index fingers on both hands displaying the letter **'W'**.

"And what's that supposed to mean?"

My gosh, this child is SLOWER than I thought.

"It means, Jasmine, 'WHATEVER!'"

She tutted and puffed at the genie's immaturity.

"I have no time for your shenanigans, Genie!"

Holding up the **'W'** sign again, he began to remind her that she only had **one** more wish left.

Five, or maybe even 10 minutes had passed on by now...

Another five minutes....

Another, perhaps 20...

"20 BLOOMIN 99!"

"Alright! Alright! I'm sure genies aren't supposed to hassle the person doing the wishing."

"I don't really care what you think, I'm not any ordinary genie, I'm a unique individual and never to be compared, FURTHERMORE! I would suggest that you think wisely about this LAST AND FINAL (Praise the Lord!!!!) wish."

Completely blocking out the genies negative energy, Jasmine tried long and hard to find herself in deep, serious though for her **last, final** wish ....
....
....
....
....
....**FINALLY!!**

She had thought of a 3rd wish.

"I've got it! I've got it!" she exclaimed excitedly, whilst jumping up and down through the air like an eager bird ready to take flight. The genie almost had a panic attack, as Jasmine had woken him out of his midday nap.

"Goodness, what year are we in now?"

Putting her hands on her hips, she shook her head at his sarcasm.

"Ha-ha! Very funny, but seriously, listen up carefully, cuz this is a good one. I wish for *'CONTINUOUS GOOD HEALTH.'*"

POOF! And it was done. Just like that.

She was fit. She was healthy. She was more than well. She felt ALIVE! She was beautiful. ☺

It was 6:00 am on a hot summer's morning and Jasmine had just been for her 2-hour morning jog. Feeling refreshed she sat on the front step of her gorgeous town house, enjoying the sunrays that graced her cheekbones invitingly. She had never felt this way before, it was better than peace, it was better than riches. It was the BEST she had felt in all her life.

Her face had suddenly frozen in deep horror as an stick like, frail and deathly pale lady walked by on her path. Her skin was saggy and carelessly hung from her body; it was an awful sight. Her eyes were bloodshot from what looked like endless nights of constant tears. Jasmine couldn't help but wonder what was wrong; she followed the lady. As she finally caught her up, she reached out, but snatched her hand back firmly.

"Excuse me, I know this may seem so rude, and I know you don't know me, however I couldn't help but notice, that you looked so sad."

The lady couldn't even look into Jasmine's face properly as if she were ashamed of her own appearance. She then began sobbing uncontrollably, tear after tear.

"Oh, if you only knew child! If you only knew! Do you even know who I am? An athlete, a great athlete. One of the best I was, one of the very best. You wouldn't believe it though, I mean look at me now, just look at me. I was so fit, so healthy, so beautiful; it was literally as if someone had sucked the life out of me. Now look at me, no one has an answer to why this has suddenly happened. No one has the answer. It's so sad; the doctor said that there is not much hope left for me now."

The old lady struggled free from Jasmine's grip, continuing on the path alone and completely miserable. Jasmine covered her mouth with her hand, as if trying to restrain herself from revealing the truth to the poor, innocent frail figure.

"Oh no! What have I done? This is all my fault."

Jasmine couldn't bear to face what she had caused; she had no intention of harming anybody else's health when she wished this wish. There was only one way she could fix such a disaster and she knew how.

Back to reality. No more wishes. It was a relief to Jasmine's traumatised mind. She contemplated on what she had experienced and what a great pleasure it was to be back to normal life all over again. She could have been forced to go to school seven days a week, subjected to money-hungry intruders every seven hours for the rest of her life or she could have destroyed the innocent life of another human being.

What a tragedy, she thought. Once again, she stood in deep thought awhile, of course not for too long with the helpful interruption of the genie.

"Well, that was fun wasn't it!" the genie chuckled whilst displaying a huge line of gleaming white teeth and high cheekbones. Jasmine looked straight back into the genie's face, and instead of retaliating to his irritating sarcasm, she simply graced him with a lovely and genuine smile.

"You know what Genie; I would like to thank you. Before meeting you I really thought my life was full of bad luck and downfalls. But after experiencing what I have experienced today, it's just made me come to the realisation that really I haven't got it that bad after all."

The genie floated puzzled and confused. Usually at the end of three wishes he expected his candidates to be miserable, but not Jasmine. He began to wonder where exactly he went wrong and if he had done his job properly this time round.

"I'm afraid I don't quite understand," he finally responded after a brief period of time of thinking to himself.

"I'm saying that 'Bad Luck' doesn't exist."

"OH!" he paused, not quite understanding Jasmine's conclusion either.

"Oh Genie! Never mind," she laughed.

Shaking his hand grippingly, she thought that she would at least attempt the last two periods of what was left of school.

"Where are you going?" the genie questioned.

"To make the most of my life!" she shouted back as she hurried along the path.

The genie glared wide-eyed as if he were in some immortal shock at Jasmine's positive attitude towards the outcome of the situation. He watched her slim, tall figure with great interrogation but not with the slightest of amusement. Sticking his tongue out after her he finally dismissed the situation holding up the 'W' sign once more.

"YOU THINK YOUR ALL THAT, BUT YOUR NOT, JASMINE KELLY!"

he bellowed aggressively after her.

"Bye Genie, don't feel discouraged, have a good life, seriously." And off she went into the distance going to make the most of life, just like she said.

Colour me in

THE FEELING OF WAR

November 1919

Dear Diary,

The feeling of war. I remember it like the days of yesteryears. How do I even begin to describe such an intense experience and life-changing journey? The endless days, the eerie nights... but most importantly, where I discovered my true strength as a *woman*.

"FLASHBACK!"

Wait. This may take a moment.

Andrea Kydd-Hope is my name. Hope. Quite a powerful last name. Hope. It was hope that made me exceedingly determined to survive the oppressive, burdensome feeling of war. It was a hope that gave me the strength, the courage and the faith to face the scornful gaze of fear. So, what is hope? A feeling of desire? A possibility of fulfilment? These are just two definitions of the word. However, I define it as the key. The key to unlock the door of a future without limits. My *limitless* future.

Look and read carefully.

This is my story. . . .

July 1916 – The Battle of the Somme

Dear Diary,

I should not be here. I feel scared and sick to the pit of my stomach, which any moment is going to regurgitate a combination of anxiety, dread and cowardice. In short, there are three reasons why I definitely should *not* be here: Brown. Woman. Defenseless. Some call me Black British, my birth certificate says NEGRO, others call me coloured, but I refer to myself as firstly, *just* Andrea, and secondly, a person who is mixed white and black, but my chocolate brown skin would convince you otherwise.

The law indicates that I, a *woman*, was an intruder on this ship, that I, a *black British woman,* was not allowed to apply to be a nurse or be recognised as a key feature in the war, so I decided to disguise myself as a man. The British army didn't know it, but my help was needed and so, I gave it. Most importantly, I believed that maybe, just maybe this could be my chance to show how wrong it was for them to reject people like me, who wanted to serve their country and receive a steady military income.

The ships progressed closer and closer towards the dominating hedgehogs that attempted to stop us from entering the restricted territories of the German forces. I watched in aberration as soldiers continuously vomited, some with consistently shaking hands, some with hands clasped together or holding their sacred crosses and praying deeply for the sake of their own lives.

Boom! Crash! Bang! The atmosphere changed, immediately contrasting dramatically to what it was 5 minutes before. It was loud and aggressive. A series of gas bombs and bullets sharply flew in my immediate direction. Soldiers panicked, moving swiftly up and down the ship. Many went overboard in an attempt to save themselves. They were so scared they forgot that they were carrying heavy luggage, ironically contributing to their own deaths as one by one they drowned. Our army was vulnerable in comparison to the powerful force of our enemies. For a split moment, the atmosphere muffled around me, I was unable to hear anything. Trudging through the glacial blood filled waters; I was diverted constantly as masses of dead bodies interfered in my path. An explosion alerted my hearing once more. Searching anxiously for cover, without hesitating I ran at a rapid pace. Knowing I couldn't stop, knowing that death was strong enough to overtake me, knowing that I wanted to survive, I knew anything was possible at this moment in time. Thinking of where I was going didn't actually once occur to me, strangely. I just had to get out of sight, and soon. Stumbling here and there over several dead bodies delayed even more of my precious time, and encouraged more of my frustration.

I absolutely have no place here.

Oh no! What was happening? The overwhelming feeling of terror struck my stomach as I watched a group of threatening figures move towards me swiftly. They were all securely armed. I clearly had no chance of survival, I thought hope had failed me; I was completely (brown, woman) defenceless against them. A great beautiful blaze of bright lights filtered through the air as they began to shoot wildly with their guns. Having no occasion to appreciate this scenery, I stopped, dropped and rolled, stretching my body to its full extent; long and tall across the ground. I was hoping to be camouflaged between whatever rubble was surrounding me. Sweat rained down my forehead like a running waterfall as I waited in the painful silence. I could no longer hear a sound, maybe it was a trap? Should I take the risk? No! Yes? I couldn't hear a sound, what was I to do? I couldn't take this anxious feeling of waiting any longer as the intrusive silence provoked me abundantly like the irritating presence of a flitting fly hitting against a window. The creak of daylight echoed against the clouds as I sat and gazed helplessly, as if crying out to the merciless skies. The impatience of my nature had grown into a sluggish manner of complete rage.

Then began the clamorous noise of the death prone targets once more. Shutting the battered, brown eyelids upon my bruised and swollen face, I began to pray desperately. The never-ending sounds increased the running pulse of my heartbeat to a rapid pace that ventured into the near motion of bursting out the delicate flesh of my agonising chest.

Here, was no place for any man or woman.

With an immediate haste, the boisterous commotion died abruptly, into the distance. The shots had finally drawn to a close. They had stopped. Gone. Vanished. Elapsed completely, with such random timing. After a substantial amount of time, thinking that the coast was now clear, I steadily got back onto my feet, and began to make my way, in an attempt to reunite myself with the rest of my troop. As I took gradual steps, my movement was cut short; something was not right. A familiar, uninviting noise made me eminently uncomfortable. I went to resume my original shelter of cover, but it was then too late. Oh no! I was wrong. I was DOOMED! In a split instant, I was suddenly greeted with the tremendous presence of a pollutant fumed gas bomb. Losing all sense of gravitational force it flew me violently in the daunting atmosphere of mid-air; landing with my spine harshly against the huge, hardened surface of a grey crinkled rock.

Am I still here?

A week later July 1916

Dear Diary,

Is it over? Please tell me it is. Maybe it is. Could it be? Maybe I'm about to be awakened from this disastrous nightmare, to be surrounded by the faces of those dearest to my heart. My dear father and mother, who don't even know I lied to them and enlisted myself in this war. I wanted so badly to be able to return home and tell them about my bravery, about what I have seen and experienced, about how I planned to change the future for women like me. At 19-years-old, there was so much more I wanted to accomplish in my life, and THIS, this was only the beginning.

I've been sitting here in the chancy war battle-field for what seems like forever in the unaccom-panied presence of myself. Tediously waiting. Just a lonely soldier. A woman at that, in obsolete condi-tions. After a horrific, barbarous bloody war.

A tidal wave of emotions have captured the depths of my confounded brain. Placing them un-derneath a heinous sluggish tide of doom, I've lost all sense of hope, determination and my fight for equality feels so far out of reach and unachievable. I feel so alone, exposed and foolish for the danger I have put myself in. I'm completely helpless at this present moment in time. I have been abandoned. Deserted. Left behind. Left to face the grim -visage, belligerent faces of my adversaries. Adversaries who despise me, my country and me even more. Adversaries who are able to take away the precious being of a life and re-claim it as their vivacious victory.

I am now facing the consequences of being here.

The gross feeling of mucilaginous mud sinks deeply through my shattered clothing, seeping into my neck, making my body wince in disgust. The hard encased material of my helmet submerges my forehead, forcefully trying to blind my vision, as I lie on my back miserable and in doubt. Yes, you could say I am in complete and utter despair AND...I can't move! I can't feel my legs or my feet or any movement in my lower body. This could not get any worse.

Disaster filled the atmosphere. Battered machinery, guns, army wear, and they all lay sporadically scattered in the distant scenery. How could I remain hopeful, if not even dead bodies were here to grace me with their presence? All I have are the tragic memories of the past week. The intimidating polluted clouds, frown down fiercely on me and tell me I will die out here and looking ahead I see nothing to convince me that they are lying. Nothing. My fate looks dark and the days ahead are too unbearable to comprehend.

How long do I have left here?

SILENCE! Not a peep. Nor a sound. All was quiet. So quiet, it provoked me to anger. The constant revisitation of howling winds pimpled my shivering skin like symptoms of severe acne. The sound continuously grew louder and louder, penetrating itself at lightning pace through the ringing dark tombs of my eardrums. Then it suddenly stopped! I began to reminisce about the raging cries. Screams and sounds of agony I once heard. It was like a never ending nightmare. Tears wet the sides of my cheeks as I began to realise the blessing bestowed upon my life, as I was still alive and waiting. I may be down, but I am not out and my story is not over.

Trying to hang on in here.

Waiting to be rescued is unnerving. The atmosphere is incredibly inconsistent, and is now completely dead and mute.

It stinks! The stench of blood is nauseating and entwines itself with the deep blackened skies. The clouds look extremely heavy in weight as they droop dramatically, almost kissing the ground. They unleash the revolting smell of toxic gases that severely sting my innocent eyes, making them shed uncontrollable anguishing tears. I cough repeatedly like in the midst of a harrowing spasm as more fumes begin to accelerate through my body piercing my insides, and cling resolutely to the back of my throat.

Gripping the ground with firm intensity, I feel the mounds of artificial banks and earth slice against fragments of my aching wrists, leaving them in more agonising pain. I start sweating heavily, as if being chased by a vicious mob of fierce warriors. Biting my once smooth, now dry, chapped lips, I try with all my might to hang on in there while I endure this intolerable and excruciating pain.

Moments later...

This atrocious experience has become more than overwhelming. It was like being phys- ically dead but emotionally alive. I wished for my grungy nail beds to render the weak flesh from my cheeks and make this all stop. Right now, I'd give anything to make it all go away.

Still waiting ....

Time passes.

Time had passed.

Time was still passing.

SI was still waiting.

I am still alive.

I AM STILL ALIVE?

I'm alive!

So, why am I still here?

Why has no one come to rescue me yet?

Was I so unimportant, so unremembered that people didn't even notice me here?

It was all just too much. I'm angry! FURIOUS! Tired of waiting. The thought that I might die a lonely soldier, a forgotten woman in war, in unfamiliar surroundings, without having a chance to see my family and friends again…is just…it's…

GET ME OUT OF HERE!

A moment of Hope…

A sharp noise entered my ears. My body is too stiff to encourage any movement in my neck to look around. I easily distinguished what the sound was as it drew closer towards me. Before my eyes, I saw a truck approaching where I had been situated miserably for days on end. I was being rescued. Finally. At last. Can you believe it? Someone had come to rescue me. Someone cared enough to ensure my survival. For the first time in my life, I felt worthy. My life did have worth. I realised that I had the right to live just as much as any other male soldier who precariously risked their life for their country. That's when I believed. I believed with all my might that 'hope' couldn't have failed me yet. It would never fail me.

I feel a hand sweep underneath my back and suddenly I am lifted into the arms of safety. It's not long before I pass out but somehow in my conscious mind, I know that Andrea Kydd-Hope, is still here.

November 1919

Dear Diary,

This experience was a defining moment in my life. I learned that you have to be careful what you wish for. I wished for this experience so I could make a change for women like me and it almost cost me my life. My life. Yet, if I was given a chance to go back in time, I would not erase a single thing. I now write sitting in a wheel chair, with an amputated left leg, but I am stronger than ever, at least in my mind. This experience taught me that I am a risk-taker, a fighter and UNSTOPPABLE. Just because I faced rejection, it didn't stop me, it could not stop me and I won! *We won.* I did it for the women of now and girls, like you, of the future. Don't ever let anybody define your worth, or tell you you're not good enough, you have the right to *BE*

HERE! And because I stood my ground, because I stood up for what I believed in, I made a change for my people. *One* 'no' couldn't stop me, and this one disability will never disable me from continuing my mission for equality. *I am here to stay!* **Brown. Woman. Resilient.**

Colour me in

SNOW BLACK

AND THE SEVEN RASTAS

F ar, far away in the hot, exotic island of Jamaica, behind the tall palm trees, beyond the white-sandy beaches and tropical waters lived a beautiful, ravishing princess known as Snow Black. Oh, and what a radiant sight she was, her skin was a smooth, dark glowing brown, like thick, creamy, rich Cadbury's chocolate. Her hair, short and soft, combed perfectly into a fluffy, light afro, decorated with a yellow rose at the side; her thick lips sparkled permanently from the sweet strawberry gloss they were coated in and her broad chocolate buttoned nose sat promptly fixed in perfect proportion with the rest of her face. She was a Coca Cola bottle figure, emphasising her thick, well rounded curves. Natural born beauty they said, neither spot nor blemish, no cosmetics, just a natural born beauty.

Unfortunately, her mother died when she was only a youngling, leaving her to fend for herself against her evil step-father. He was scornful and despised Snow Black. He mistreated her severely day by day, locking her away in the dark, deserted, unknown depths of the black dungeon, feeding her tiny crumbs of stale hardo bread and a few sips of coconut water. Oh, how she pleaded for his mercy, how she wanted to flee and never return.

Many years passed on by this time, and Snow Black had grown, even more, into one of the most, elegant, desirable ladies ever seen. As she rose from her bedside gracefully each morning, she was greeted with the joyful tune of birds singing in sweet unison. Nature adored her very presence, her sweet smelling scent and gleaming smile warmed their hearts. She was banished from the sight of her evil step-father, so she spent her days writing creatively in her trusted journal or sitting on the wide ledge of her window, staring yearningly out towards the rich blue skies, watching the white furry cushions as they sat within it, slowing passing by. She only hoped and prayed every single second that something or someone would come to her rescue, and sweep her out of sight, as far away from her evil step-father as she could get, away into a land filled with happiness.

"Mirror! Mirror! Pon de wall! A whu da most gud looking nest of dem all?"

This was the repetitive phrase that the evil step-father never ceased to boom at the colossal mirror hanging lamentably on the wall each day. The mirror would then reply by saying, "Bwoi sah, yu luk good, but Snow Black luk betta dan yu man!"

"Mi back foot! Yu lie! Yu lie! A wah yu a say, yu a tek bad tings mek joke!"

"No man, a nuh lie mi a tell, a true, a true!"

The evil step-father would burn with fury and envy at Snow Black's beauty when he heard this response. His patience could no longer be tested any further; he had had enough. It was not long after that he requested that Snow Black be killed.

When Snow Black heard such horrific news, she was overwhelmed tremendously with fear and anxiety. It was then that she built up the determination that she must escape. Her evil step-father's actions had left her no choice. She didn't want to die, and refused to give him the satisfaction. She ran and ran, far, far away into the deep, shadowy depths of the territorial Yam-Yam forest. She ran for hours, as far as her stylish gladiator sandals could carry her. She carried on running, maybe a day or two, but she refused to stop until she was certain that she was safe, and not until she knew she was as far away as possible.

Now during this particular moment in Jamaica, the weather had brought the most unexpected gift. Snow? Yes, snow indeed. Snow Black adored the very essence, she loved the presence of snow. The trees shared their white coats openly as they bowed forthwith as if inviting Snow Black into their palm leaves for warmth. The ground carried her feet carefully as they soaked her footprints in remembrance. It was a gift especially for her.

Eventually, after such a tiresome and seemingly never ending journey she discovered an extravagant, elaborate mansion. The silver gates shone radiantly in the sharp horizon. The scorching yellow substance lying succulently waiting, in a blue embedded duvet of white cushions, reflected its surface, whilst slowly causing the snow to disappear. These were the superior gates that held the elegant entrance to what beheld prestigious courts. Something new. Something different. Something unique. The mansion was coated in a metallic gold paint as it towered high, standing so tall and wide as if defining that this territory only belonged to itself, and it alone. It was surrounded with a humongous banquet of luscious plantation such as yellow daffodils, purple hyacinths, blue tulips, pink carnations, white lilies, red roses and numerous rows of ital herbs. They were all planted perfectly in columns and rows standing graciously upright in position. Snow Black questioned to herself how it was even possible for them to survive due to the conditions they were in. They stood along the hedges of the green marbled pathway, detailed with the fine intricate décor of crystallised sequences of multi-coloured gems that sparkled like glowing stars. The path was long and regal like the entry to the red carpet, but without the extreme, bright flashes of white lights.

When the seemingly never ending path had drawn to a close, before her stood a huge door. The door to the inside was beautifully two-toned with shades of brown; ecru, a greyish-pale yellow and russet, a brown colour with a reddish tinge. It had two large golden handles on the left and right, along with a matching gold bell that played a sweet harmonious tune when rung.

Beyond the doors lay the foundation of luxurious quarters. Vibrant colours lit the atmosphere from the ceiling to the polished tiled floors, which reflected the image of every object in its view with perfect accuracy. The atmosphere was alive, warm and inviting. The walls were covered in a mustard yellow that smiled brightly. Moving on further began the entrance to the tranquil living area. Its sense of peace and purity was enough to refresh the state of a stressful mind; everything that it contained sat in a gentle nature. There were white fluffy sofas that were so deep that an infant's body would be able to sink into its stomach comfortably. White cushions of all different shapes and sizes filled the sofas; some were also laid neatly around the edges of the room.

To the left of this room was an opulent dining area. It contained a long glass table which looked delicate enough to break with the tap of a fingernail. Above it was a majestic silver chandelier that hung in a dignified fashion; high and proud. The table was laid with clear wine glasses and the lustrous sheen of sterling silver cutlery in precise order.

"Coo yah, de place luk gud!" she exclaimed breathlessly. She had never seen such a wonderful sight in all her days.

Without further ado or hesitant reaction, she wanted to see more. A complete stranger, completely oblivious to where she was, she stood in amazement at her surroundings. Searching the site of the complex house, she had no intention of leaving without seeing all the rooms, or at least gracing them with her presence. Excitement bloomed throughout her like a bunch of flower buds opening in the season of spring. It was a memorable moment, maybe the best moment in her life so far.

"A wah dis?" she questioned while picking up an old Bob Marley record she found lying on a large case, full of other various records.

"Buffalo Soldier! Woi, dis a mi jam, man!"

She immediately placed the record onto the glamorous, silver, record player that she had seen in the corner of the room. Snow Black danced and danced around for hours on end, doing tasteless, vulgar actions such as the Butterfly, the Bogle, the Shelly Belly, and even the Dutty Wine. Was this even legal, you may ask? Of course it was, just harmless fun in the eyes of Snow Black, who at this point in time couldn't have given a single care in the world whether it was legal or not.

Meanwhile back at the palace, Snow Black's evil step-father was absolutely furious that she had managed to escape so quickly and easily, even after all the traps he had set to make sure that this was impossible. He knew that she had grown too smart for him now, he tried to devise a plan to be rid of her once and for all; but until one came to mind, for the time being, he would send out a search party of seven hundred soldiers to find her.

"FINE ER! FINE ER," he ordered. "MI NUH BUSINESS IF SHE DEAD OR ALIVE! AN NUH BADDA CUM BACK WIDOUT HER!"

Back at the luxurious mansion, Snow Black had become overly exhausted after releasing some serious energy from dancing for so long. Ready for a rest, she ran up the delicate steps of the grand glass staircase, to find a choice of seven large bedroom suites appear before her very eyes. Which one to choose? It was such a difficult decision, all of them were so beautiful, minus the fact that they all contained ash-trays. However, she finally brought herself to choose one. The suite she had chosen was all white, from the ceiling, to the carpet, even the furniture and the quilt covers! It was such a tranquil environment to be in, she fell in love with the feeling it gave to her. Before shutting her eyes to partake in a brief beauty rest, she couldn't help but wonder to herself, "Whu wudda need seven large bedroom suites?"

Yawning with a triumphant noise, she fell fast into a deep, peaceful sleep.

Many seconds turned into minutes, which then turned into hours. By now, Snow Black was in a deep, peaceful sleep. For such a beautiful princess, her sleeping manners were not as graceful. She was completely ignorant as to what was going on around her. By now, it hadn't even occurred to her that she had been trespassing in the home of seven Rastas until ….

"A WHU DIS IN A MI BLARSTED BED, TU BACKSIDE?!"

With that, the rest of them came rushing in.

"Kekeh, what a feisty pickney eeh, yuh shud trow er out a door!"

Suddenly, in the blink of an eye, Snow Black awoke to face the astonished facial expressions of seven complete strangers all staring directly at her.

"Aah! Come out mi face, nuh!" howled Snow Black.

"Backfoot! A dupey! A dupey!"

She jumped straight out the bed within an instant, holding a pillow that partially covered her startled face as some sort of defence; she didn't know what to do with herself.

"Whey mi deh? A who yuh?" she questioned.

"Chu nah gyal, yuh nearly mek me have a heart attack, yuh in wei yard to backfoot, we shud be askin you de same ting."

With a quick interruption, the other Rastas were so mesmerised at Snow Black's unique beauty that they zoomed past to get a good and closer look at her.

"Ooh gyal, yuh luk gud, man!"

"Yeh man, yuh luk fresh!"

"Real nice!"

"Mek me luk pan yuh face... WOI!"

"Whu yuh? Whu yuh? Whu yuh?" Snow Black asked and asked once again. The attention became flustering.

Suddenly, one of the Rastas began to beat box, then joined in another with humming, then another with patting a rhythmic tune on his knee, then another with clicking. Then began the singing.

"Well mi name is one, Ziggy, an mi love fi jiggy. Dis a two, Reggae. Three, Rum. Four, Pumpkin. An dat a five, Dumplin, 'im Chickin is finga lickin. Den yuh hav six, Tom-Tom. An las but no least yuh hav seven, Big-bwoi an im caan eats sah!"

After introducing themselves in such an unusual choice of song, it was then that Snow Black started to feel more at ease.

"An wha shud we call yuh mi darlin'?"

"Snow Black, mi name is Snow Black."

"Snow Black, wat a pretty name, eeh!" Ziggy exclaimed.

"An is wat bring yuh so far into de deep, depths of Yam Yam Forest?"

"Mi so so sorry, but mi caan explain for intruding in all yuh yard. Mi hav waan wicked step-father yuh sei, an im wan fi kill mi, so mi ha fi escape."

"Coo yah im wan fi kill yuh, im wicked man!"

"Mi knuw, dats why mi ere."

The seven Rastas were very sympathetic towards Snow Black's situation, although she was a complete stranger and, realistically, a trespasser.

Meanwhile, back at the palace, the evil-step father had eventually been notified of where Snow Black currently was. Killing her the way he first intended would be much too hard, so he devised an even better plan of how to be rid of her once and for all. This time, his scheming idea was cunning and sneaky; he decided to send out one of his royal assistants disguised as a sweet elderly lady. He then gave the royal assistant a bottle of poisoned ginger beer to give to Snow Black. The bottle was wrapped decoratively with pink and yellow ribbon and a humongous silver bow just to top it off tastefully. His only wish was to outsmart Snow Black one day and he actually believed that this was going to work.

However, back at the luxurious mansion, the seven Rastas had made Snow Black feel at home. They welcomed her wholeheartedly into their home to stay as long as she needed. To celebrate her arrival, they had cooked up a big, scrumptious banquet of Caribbean dishes. There was ackee and saltfish, curry goat, jerk chicken, barbeque chicken, lobster, crab, rice and peas, fried dumpling, plantain, sweet potato, yam, pumpkin, hardo bread, patties, festival, macaroni cheese, fry fish and run-dung, blue draaws, cow cock soup, stew peas and much, much more. It was a mighty, wondrous and delicious feast, never to be forgotten. Snow Black ate so fast that she drew the immediate attention of the seven Rastas as they watched her literally clean the whole table. To their amazement they would have never have thought her appetite would be so big with her having such a slim-lined figure. She had eaten so much her belly became overly bloated, causing a button to pop off her dress.

"Woi sah! Yu sure can cook Dumpling, tank yuh ever so much," she said in a very appreciative manner.

"Tank yu mi darlin', anytime, anytime," he smiled in response.

After a game of limbo and musical statues, the seven Rastas had to leave awhile to plant crops and some more ital herbs in their fields. They left Snow Black sitting cosily by the fire in a rather large mustard coloured rocking chair. She sat happily whilst humming joyful tunes to herself. She had never felt so happy in all her life; it was the experience of freedom.

Her ears were then alerted as there was a loud knock on the door. She assumed it would be Big-bwoi coming back for more food. She opened the door, not knowing the precarious situation she was about to enter into. To her surprise, a sweet looking elderly lady stood before her eyes. She was very petite and looked fragile; she wore a navy blue frock patterned in tropical flowers, along with eccentric pearl earrings, necklace and bracelet.

"Hello mi darlin'," greeted the elderly lady.

"Hello mam, wah caan mi duh fi yuh?"

"Well mi was jus passin' through de forest and mi cum across dis beautiful mansion dat did stand out from afar, so mi taught mi shud bring sum ginger beer cum as a gift for de person who own it."

"Oh how kind of yuh mam, tank yuh very much an God bless." Snow Black smiled gently at the sweet elderly lady's generosity while retrieving the poisonous bottle right from her very hands.

"You're welcome mi darlin', an mi shud be off now, take care."

"Okay, bye mam."

Snow Black couldn't help but admire the lovely decorating on the bottle; she also couldn't help but admire the fact that the elderly lady had been so kind. However, Snow Black did find it a bit strange that an elderly lady was wandering around and about in the deep, territorial depths of Yam Yam Forest by herself. Oh well, that wasn't the point was it, the point was there was still some good left in the world and if the elderly lady wanted to be so generous then who was Snow Black to question this. She poured the contents carefully into a large glass making sure that she didn't spill a drop, she wasn't about to let any of this ginger beer go to waste. Gulping it down quickly, she loved the lingering sweet taste it left on the tip of her tongue. She had a craving; she poured another glass, then another, and then impatiently she just drank the rest from the bottle itself.

"Woi sah dat was nice man!"

THUD!

In an instant, Snow Black fell to the ground. No, she was not dead like the evil step-father had intended, however she was unconscious from the poisoned drink.

Moments later, the seven Rastas had returned from the fields and were horrified to see Snow Black lying stiffly sprawled out on the living room floor.

"Oh, Lard God! A wah happen to she?" panicked Pumpkin as he walked round in circles on himself.

"Snow Black! Snow Black! Wake up nuh, man! A wah wrong wid yuh?" cried Ziggy.

"Snow Black, yuh dead?" shouted Reggae.

"NOOO!!!" bawled Dumplin.

The seven Rastas did everything in their power to try and wake up the damsel in distress. They tried to resuscitate her, they tried playing loud music, and they even threw the remains of mutton gravy on her face. It was no use; there was not a single word, action nor response from Snow Black. They had to accept the situation that was at hand, once and for all. The fact of the matter was Snow Black was dead and there was nothing they could do about it. Whether they had chosen to accept this was a different matter altogether.

After moments of awkward silence...

"Well sah, we cyaan jus leave her deh suh jus sprawl out sprawl out pon de floor like dis," said Tom–Tom, whilst dabbing the mutton gravy off Snow Black's face with a damp paper towel.

"I'm right man, we hav fi bury er," suggested Big-bwoi while munching quickly on a piece of tasty jerk chicken leg.

Within three days, the seven Rastas had built Snow Black a glass coffin. Their blood, sweat and tears went into it; literally. It sparkled lustrously in the bright morning sunshine. They placed in it primroses and daises, then carefully, Snow Black's tender body was placed in the centre of it. They carried her to the fields where they had prepared the funeral ceremony. Dumplin nearly dropped the coffin on the way as he was mourning for the loss of Snow Black. He was not alone in this, as it was too much for all of them to bear. It was so strange, as they were mourning for a person they barely even knew, but they knew that Snow Black had a good heart. They were all dressed in fluorescent suits patterned with the Jamaican flag; they also wore black sunglasses to block out the blazing sun from their faces. As they arrived onto the fields, they placed the coffin down and proceeded with the service. They all comforted themselves with ital herbs so the pain of Snow Black's death wouldn't hurt so badly. Each of them paid a little tribute in her memory. After this a moment of silence was held as the song 'Three Little Birds' by Bob Marley was played in the background. The Rastas sobbed and bawled to their hearts content, Big-bwoi blew his nose; loudly startling Pumpkin who was beside him. Yes, this was their moment of silence.

As the special service drew to a close, Snow Black's coffin was placed vertically, down onto a wooden platform on the ground; they had decided not to bury her properly, for such beauty should never be hidden away. They said their final goodbyes and farewells and off they all went, still in mourning.

"Noo! Noo! Mi cyaan leave she! Mi cyaan do it!" cried Dumplin.

"Cum on man, tap de cow bawling! Yuh hav no choice." Rum and Reggae had to drag Dumplin away from the scene as he was making an exhibition of himself.

A moment had passed, and it was not long after that a mighty, strapping black beauty had galloped into sight. Its exquisite long black hair shimmered in the sunlight as a handsome muscular young prince stepped off the horse. He stood still, fazed by Snow Black's beauty and hovered gently over her coffin. He had never seen someone so beautiful in all his days. His heartbeat accelerated as he drooled at her side.

"What a pretty gyal sah!"

Cautiously he opened the glass lid of the coffin. Completely dazzled and delighted he took hold of her body in his masculine biceps, holding it so close to his chest that his heart may have just skipped a beat, it was then that he kissed her lips passionately, savouring each second of the sensational, romantic taste. Snow Black instantly arose from her state of unconsciousness, their eyes locked intimately as they warmed each other's hearts smoothly with their gasping breaths of love and affection. It was, yes indeed, love at first sight.

"Oh so handsome! So…so…Oh, where hav u bin all mi life man?" Snow Black questioned devotedly. The prince chuckled casually at her question; he then drew her closer till there was not a single gap between them. Looking deep into her eyes as he held her hands against his chest, he asked fervently. "What is yuh name darlin'?"

"Snow Black."

"Snow Black yuh are mi true love, marry me?"

Astonished by such an unexpected proposal, all her dreams had suddenly started to unlock from the hidden places they once harboured. She had waited for this moment all her life and it was finally here, it was finally here.

"YES! YES! I WILL!" Her only reply could have been yes, and with that the prince took Snow Black's hand in his and as she arose from her coffin delicately, he held her in his arms with a firm grip as if he was never going to let her go.

Up from the distance came running the seven Rastas as they saw the moving figures from afar.

"SNOW BLACK! IT CAAN'T BE! YUH ALIVE! TANK DE LARD YUH ALIVE CHILD!" shrieked Ziggy.

They all flung their arms around her giving her the greatest loving hug. She hugged them back willingly, whilst tear drops of joy streamed from her eyes.

"Tank yuh for everyting!"

"Wah yuh mean, oh no Snow Snow, yuh goin, oh why? Oh why?" whimpered Reggae.

"Yuh jus not too long cum bac from di dead!" snuffled Pumpkin.

"Oh, please stay!" pleaded Rum.

Her heart became overwhelmed with sadness and guilt for the Rastas, as she knew that not even she really wanted to leave them either. She could never forget how kind and loving they were towards her. I mean how many people would take a complete stranger into their home, feed and nurture her? However, she knew she had a life to lead, beyond Yam-Yam Forest, and she wanted to see it for herself. She had been awaiting this moment her whole life and there was just no stopping her now, she was going to take it and run with it.

"Don't worry, mi never ever goin' to forget unu, never, I promise, an I will cum bac an visit yuh all once mi sekkle." She gave them all one last hug, and kisses on the sides of their tearful, wet cheeks.

"We will miss yuh darling, Snow Black," they waved and sobbed as she took her position on the back of the black beauty with her new husband to be.

"I will miss yuh too Ziggy, Reggae, Rum, Pumpkin, Dumplin, Tom-Tom and Big-Bwoi, an once agen, tank unu for everyting."

Off she galloped with her handsome prince. Far, far away into a land and life of eternal happiness going to fulfil the destiny that awaited her.

Colour me in

WILL YOU BE MY VALENTINE?

Thursday 14 February

Dear Diary,

Can you believe it's Valentine's Day and I still don't have a boyfriend! It's a joke. It a cliché anyway. It doesn't mean anything, but try telling that to all these people around me flashing their cheesy cards around, wondering who their secret admirers are. I bet they knew really, half of them probably sent them to themselves, like I did. Sad I know, but I couldn't bear the embarrassment of all my friends having one apart from me. Tiana got 13 cards (LUCKKY for her!), Kam got 7 and Kay got 3, I don't know how that one works. Kamera and Kayla are identical twins, they practically look exactly alike; if anything, it's strange that Kam received more cards. But who cares! The point is I received 0, nought, zilch! It's so not fair.

I mean it's not that I need a boyfriend, I just have a serious case of FOMO (fear of missing out). Dad says, "What do you need a boyfriend at your age for? Be careful not to grow up too quickly Marnie. Besides boys have very contagious germs, and if you catch them now they don't heal until you're 35!"

I wouldn't call myself an academic, but we all know this is Dad talk for 'I want you to stay my little girl, foreveeeeerrr."

My Mom died when I was 6-years-old, so Dad has had to be both parents to me and my little (annoying) brother, Logan. I love him, but he's STILL annoying. Anyway, Dad has been great at raising us and has never made out like it's been harder to understand me than Logan just because I'm a girl, but the first time we had our conversation about boyfriends, it's like he froze in time...No I mean literally; he spaced out for like 10 seconds staring out the window. I get that he's my Dad and I'm his only daughter, yada yada yada, but I'm also 14, with feelings, who takes at least 20 selfies at a time and currently has a love-hate relationship with social media...**Don't you see?** I'm practically on the brink of WOMANHOOD!

My friends were all blushing...it was so cringe! Like really? I just CAN'T with them right now. Plus they're being hella annoying by asking me rhetorical questions like, "Do you really think I have secret admirers Marnz?" Yeah, right, like I'm really supposed to know the answer to that, what do they want me to do, take handwriting samples from each of the cards and do some sort of weird scientific investigation with them, in order to identify the culprits that wrote them? **Newsflash!** I do have a life, #thankunext!

AND furthermore! Who on earth sends cards in 2019? Is this the 1950s or something? LOOONG! The last time I remembered, if you like someone, you just follow them on IG, like a few pictures, maybe comment, so they deffo get the hint and then DM them...But a card?! Yep, they definitely wrote those cards to themselves like I did. SMH.

TBF, I just want today to be over! Tyler Wilson is having a house party this weekend; he's invited a majority of the year group including me, Tee, Kam and Kay. **Newsflash** again! You would never guess who is going to be at that party too, OMD! OMDDD! I can't even say his name...Say his name, say his name! ASHLEY WILLIAMS IS BAE!! I can't even... Guurrll! Edges snatched. **BREATHE**, it's okay...I'm okay! In my eyes he is sooo FIIYAH. I know, he's just a boy (please don't judge me) but babe, listen, I cannot exaggerate or make these things up. Tee, Kam and Kay don't see the big deal about him, but they all CLEARLY need their eyesight testing. Let's just say we differ in taste, Tee likes skinny guys, Kam doesn't have a type and Kay loves the smart ones, who have to be able to play at least one instrument, go to church and feel just as strongly about animal rights as she does...Not much to ask for at 14! But anyway, back to the subject of Ashley, I gotta GLOW all the way UP for this partaaay! Even if we don't get to talk, he needs to at least notice me.

We've spoken like once, and I doubt he even remembers my name. It's not that I'm forgettable, I'm just not as in his face as other girls. I'm not that desperate for attention, but I like him and well... I guess it would be nice to have him sorta, kinda, like me back. I'm also not superficial, it's not just his looks (and dreamy smile) that almost hypnotise me; it's his mannerisms. I may be young, but I'm no young, dumb teen. My Dad taught me about how a guy is supposed to treat me and Ashley is so polite, like real nice, like real, real gentlemen polite. It's like he's secretly 30 and somehow aged backwards. Some people will say he's cheesy, but it's different, it makes him different from the rest. My type of BF. What to wear? What to wear?

I can't do this now. I'm going to decide tomorrow when the girlies come over. For every event without fail, our priorities are to help each other choose the perfect outfits. It's essential in a girl's life to have friends that know what looks great on you and what can end up making you look like The Grinch. I mean, don't get me wrong, I have quite a good eye when it comes to fashion and style, but the odd opinion or in my friend's case, approvals won't hurt.

Hang on: I'm sensing something looking over my shoulders.

"LOGAAAN! GET OUUUT!"

Sorry, little brothers. I think it's a sign, I'm going to hide you now Diary, I'll attend to you again tomorrow when intruding eyes are far away.

Downstairs

Partaking in my usual daily routine of having vanilla ice-cream with crushed digestives biscuits at precisely 5:37pm... Oh no! And the unfortunate events just kept on coming ...

"DAAAD! WHAT ARE YOU DOING?"

He stands frozen, completely caught in the act. As if he really thought I wouldn't catch him trying to sneak MY ice-cream out the kitchen.

They say bad things happen to you in 3s, please, please, please Lord, spare me!

Back in my bedroom

Hmmm... Tossing and turning...hmmmmmm.

It's no use, I can't possibly sleep, not like this, I'm anxious about this party. Like, I'm over thinking everything. It really isn't that DEEP, but I'm a low-key perfectionist (control freak), who likes things to go the way I plan in my mind. I just need to look great, feel amazing, get noticed and have a good time. SIMPLE.

Saturday 16 February

This is the day! It's here! It's here! OMD! It's actually here. Teeth brushed – check; face washed – check; showered – check; prayed – double check! Gargled mouth wash...I KNEW I forgot something!

At 3:00pm, I start getting ready, hair and

make-up takes considerably long as it's not my calling so I follow online tutorials on YouTube. I hate looking caked so I'm going for a 'less is more' look... plus I don't want any foundation marks to find themselves on my clothes...not tonight, it needs to be PERFECT.

By 4:00pm, the girlies were round with a suitcase full of options for outfits. This, is going to be a LONG afternoon.

Two hours pass, and we're finally all ready. Tee has the best long legs ever, she's wearing black skinny jeans and a multi-coloured cropped hoody, Kam is Queen of glam and tonight is dazzling us in a super cute red glittery off the shoulder dress, Kay is wearing, a T-shirt that says 'Say no to animal testing!'...I know! Don't. Say. A. Word.

Finally, me... I don't know why I'm always left until last. Well you know the saying 'Save the best until last,' and that's exactly what they were doing, because no doubt I was going to look the best tonight. After a long attentive time of making me an exquisite sight of perfection, I would say we all had produced a beautiful on point look for the party. I wore a sassy short black dress that complimented my curvy waistline, topped off with a pair of knee high boots (that I had to hide from Dad because he'd deffo freak if he knew what I was in tonight – please **DO NOT** try this at home!)

Who's ready to go?

At the party

The bus took aaggeesss and we nearly froze in our outfits. Who told us to leave home without jackets? By the time we got to Tyler's street, music was blasting so loudly we could practically feel the Earth moving under our feet:

"SHE SAY, "DO YOU LOVE ME?" I TELL HER, "ONLY PARTLY" I ONLY LOVE MY BED AND MY MOMMA, I'M SORRY."

TUUUNE! We all sang, shouting hideously out of tune at the top of our lungs, but we didn't have a care in the world. It was our night, and we were going to make the most of it.

Back in my bedroom

Dear Diary,

IT WAS AWFUL!!!

AWFULLY AMAZING!!!! ☺

Everyone was there apart from ASHLEY! Well, to begin with. I was more than disappointed at first, but I couldn't show it and give the girlies any satisfaction of saying the famous words of 'I told you so!' So I completely surprised them and had a blast! In fact, I was in the middle of the dance floor most of the night, dancing away like there was no tomorrow; I even did the karaoke four times! 'Drake – In My Feelings' definitely went down the best, I was so much in my own feelings; I meant every word. I don't drink because: 1. I'm under age and, 2. It tastes disgusting, but I really could have done with a sip of something!

Kam had to drag me away from the Karaoke machine and said I was embarrassing myself.

"OKAY! We get it, you're in your feelings but stop hogging the mic, we want to put some real music on."

I immediately snapped back, "YOU CAN BE SUCH A MEAN PRAT AT TIMES!"

I then went onto to tell her that she wasn't my Mom and didn't have the right to tell me what to do AND if she wanted to be a granny for the night then she was more than welcome to, but I was going to have FUN. After shouting my views and publicly humiliating one of my best friends, I ran outside and burst into tears. Why did I bring my Mom up and why was I so upset? The outdoor breeze was blowing some sense back into my brain, and I knew I needed to go and apologise to Kam. Just as I turned to go inside...A familiar face stood in front of me. ASHELEEEY!

"Marnie, what are you doing out here on your ones?"

"I-I-I..." Speak mouth, speak! I was distracted by his black hair, with smooth waves, his dreamy smiles that made the dimples in BOTH of his cheeks pop to perfection. I'm so done with this...

"I like you!" Wait! That was not supposed to come out my mouth. Shut up mouth, Sssh!

Remember how I said unfortunate events come in 3s, I think this is 3!

I began fidgeting, stroking my palms and twitching, my stiff fingers paralysed from the cold. My knees became weak, so weak I stumbled, nearly falling to the ground. Ashley grabbed hold of my arm, helping me to keep my balance. As he did, our eyes met and it was a MOMENT; he smiled at me, but something was different about this smile, and I smiled back.

"To be honest, I didn't think you'd be interested in someone like me."

"WHAAT? Are you okay? Have you seen yourself?" My mouth...It has NO filter today, **what is wrong with me?**

"LOOOL! You're funny!"

"Hehe". #awkwaard

He looked at me again, no smile...

"I like you too."

Just like that. Cool, calm, collected. #nofuss

I CANNOT believe that all this time, I was working myself up for someone who already noticed me! What a relief. And the best thing is, before this dress, before these boots, Ashley liked me, as in the real me, just for me! He liked me as I am. I didn't need to change or impress him or become someone I wasn't. I learned a valuable lesson tonight, and that was "I like me just the way I am (and so does Ashley)".

"MARNZ! Here you are, we've been..." Kam stops as if she's seen a ghost and stares at Ashley, behind her came Tee and Kay, who looked just as surprised.

"Err, I think I hear Tyler calling me," Tee stalls in order to remove herself from the situation.

"Erm, I think I'll go with her," Kam closely follows behind.

"Erm, I need to pee," and off Kay ran too.

We got the picture.

"Forgive my friends. They can be so awkward at times."

"Nah, it's cool! They seem like good people!"

The cold swept up my spine and chilled me; I should have known better than to wear a dress in the month of February. Without even realising it, my head somehow ended up on Ashley's shoulder and for some reason my eyes closed for a moment. Waking myself up instantly, I almost slapped myself back to reality. I also had Dad's angry eyebrows in my head, "NO BOYS MARNZ! Remember their germs."

"I would like you to meet my Dad."

"What?"

"I mean, my Dad is a cool guy. It's just him, me and my brother. He's totally cool with me having friends over, so you should come over sometime to meet him."

"Sure!"

Okay I lied, I'm only allowed female friends over, but my Dad will be fine once I convince him that Ashley is just a "study buddy".

"You look cold, here, take this."

With that he took his hoody off, and placed it around me. It felt warm and smelt like Lynx body spray.

"I don't like you because of your looks…"

This was going so well until now.

"I mean, obvs you're pretty…"

Thank God!

"But…I like you even more because you're confident, smart and FUNNY!"

"Aww, that's so sweet of you…You're not bad yourself."

Tonight was PERFECT!

It was 10.30pm before the girlies came back outside, **again,** telling me that it was time to go before angry parents started yelling down mobile phones at them. Truthfully I knew they were right, but deep down I really didn't want to leave, I wanted to stay with Ashley and talk about nothing; I just loved being in his company. He made me smile; he was actually interested in me as a person and not just what I look like.

"Well I guess I have to get going then."

"Really, how you getting home? My Dad's comin' for me at 11:00 if you wanna lift?"

"No. No. I'll be fine; really, I don't want to leave my friends." He turned to them and said "Make sure she gets home safely." They frowned at him weirdly as if they couldn't believe that he was actually giving them orders for me, their best friend. He told me to keep his jacket. Aaah, I know! I know! It's hanging on the back of my door right now; I hope his Lynx smell doesn't fade.

WAIT...There's more!!

As I turned to finally leave with a simple hug and goodbye, he asked for my number and then in a split second, BAM...The moment of magic happened; Ashley Wiliams kissed me full frontal on the lips. I think I had definitely taken flight out of Earth's atmosphere. This was definitely the most PERFECT night everrrrrr!!!!!!!!!!!!!!!. =)

Okay, so I exaggerate, it was really just a tiny peck, but still...It meant EVERYTHING!

Sunday 17th February

Dear Diary,

I can't stop thinking about last night. I had a 4-way phone call with the girls today, and they told me how I practically nearly fell over after a tiny (BIG) kiss. All that time thinking that I would stay single in my teens and never have a boyfriend has all changed in the space of days. Wow! It's like this isn't even real. Is this really happening to me?

"SOMEBODY PINCH ME!!!" …

"OW THAT ACTUALLY HURT! LOGAAAN YOU LITTLE ANNOYING PEST! GET OUT! GET OUT! GET OUT! "

ARRRRRRRRRRRRGGGHHH, Little brothers! I swear I want to ARGGGGGGH him sometimes.

Back to Ashley. I didn't get much sleep last night. In fact, I didn't sleep a wink; I was too busy thinking about the party and what happened and, AND, I can't stop talking about it, but I need to, I don't want to look like I've been waiting for this nearly half my secondary school life (which I kinda have). But I've got to calm down, before I drive myself cray cray! Too late. Okay, I'm soo tired and officially going to sleep now. Marnie exits at 2pm in the afternoon.

Night Diary

x

Monday 18th February, 4.16pm

Dear Diary,

AAAAAAAAAAAAAAAAAHH!! GUESS WHAT! GUESS WHAT! GUESS WHAT!

Soooooooooo, I got a message from Ashley saying, and I quote: "I really liked hanging out with you at the party. Will you go out with me?"

So that means you can officially call me Mrs. Ashley Williams ;) Okay, so I'll admit I need to calm down. I'm only 14! BUT...This was the BEST belated Valentine's surprise eveeeerrrr, can't wait to tell my girls!

Goodnight. Nighty, Night. xxxxxxxxxxxxxx

Colour me in

REALITY CHECK

As a child, did you watch all those children's films and cartoons about fantasy this, and fantasy that? I know I certainly did. It seemed so fascinating, so exciting, and so real. However, as you grew older all that exciting fantasy life was suddenly burst like a big bubble into a basket of flames as you discovered that it was only a figment of your imagination. A shame really, I know.

I'm Jane by the way, Jane Pip. And do you want to know a little secret? Well, do you? I don't think you're really, truly ready for what I'm about to reveal to you. Listen carefully and listen well, because information like this isn't commonly told. Fantasy Land is real! It's not just some silly old made-up, kiddy stuff like grownups always describe it to be. It's real, I tell you, and I know exactly what you're thinking. Well, how would I know, right? I know because I've been there, there and back again, seen it all with my own two brown irises and bought the t-shirt too. It's real!

Now obviously, I know that I can't just exclaim such a bizarre sounding fact and not even tell you the story, or else where would the proof be? Besides, without the story it's hard to even begin to imagine such a place.

I think you are very unaware of the incredible lifetime experience that you are about to embark on. I guarantee you; you'll have never heard anything like it. Once in a lifetime opportunity this is, and if I were you I wouldn't miss it for the world.

So may I suggest you sit back awhile, grab a blanket if needs be, maybe a biscuit or two and most importantly, enjoy...

The story begins

Jane Pip, not your average everyday ordinary school-girl, but more along the lines of a very 'unique' individual. She's a frizzy red head, tall, with a plump figure, big brown eyes that would never fail to misread a word on a page and glasses always worn on the tip of her pointy nose. Yep, she was pretty much different alright. She was never the sociable type, in fact, she was very socially awkward. But what most people didn't realise, is that her social awkwardness was never intentional, it was because she was *highly sensitive*. This means there were certain things in her surroundings that could easily overwhelm her like BIG LOUD NOISES, *scaary videos or* **stinky** smells. So, Jane preferred to spend her time alone, *reading. Yes, I said reading!* ... and sometimes, when no one was looking, she liked to pretend she was a beauty vlogger. *However*, reading remained Jane's number one passion because she loved to imagine and make things up... I mean, let's face it, reality is *overrated!*

On her way to school at a bright, early start of 8:00am, she was in a hurry to be first at the school library. Yes, I said library! Now stop with the 21 questions! Just before the 8:55am bell, the signal of another wonderful insight to more reading in the world of Jane Pip, she wanted to refresh her mind full of words, phrases, complex, compound and simple sentences to alert and activate the brain before it was diluted with the noisome racket of her classmates.

The library, her personal sanctuary, was fairly large and bright, filled with books calling her left, right and centre to read them; most importantly it was quiet just the way she liked it. As she entered through the white double doors, the room automatically welcomed her presence as if it expected her. The librarians greeted her with the usual sharp grins and energetic waves as they did each morning, showing her the new stock they were about to have in, and giving her sneak preview copies before the rest of the school even had access to them. They favoured her greatly as they saw great potential in her character.

They had never seen a person with such enduring, passionate enthusiasm to read. They had never met a student quite like her, not even remotely close which is why they were so fond and so keen to encourage her to always be herself, despite how odd and unsociable people thought she was. She resumed her usual place of comfort where she always sat to read, right in the corner of the library where she was hidden, hidden away from eyes, voices, and people. She was in a corner where she was able to think and imagine aloud without judgement; she was in a place where she could hide away from reality awhile. Her mind always liked to wander at every given opportunity into a place where only Jane could go, and that was her corner for doing this. She had brought along with her a pile of books, stacked high; she could be extremely indecisive from time to time. After some time, she had put several books aside; she was now down to the top three. This included a non-fiction, a novel and a fiction book; they were all completely different. Additionally all of them were looking like considerably interesting reads. Finally coming to a decision, she made the biased approach that she was going to choose the book that she was going to read by sight and not by content. This instantly eliminated the novel and the non-fiction book, leaving the fiction book to remain. She was attracted to its resplendent covering, and ornate fonts that leaped excitedly from the page in rejoicing motion because Jane had picked it. Its title read. 'Fantasy', relevant to what Jane intended to do that very morning: fantasise. Turning the book to the back, she wanted to get an insight to what 'Fantasy' was about. Strangely, it contained one sentence stating, 'I think you are very unaware of the incredible life-time experience that you are about to embark on.' Jane found this very unusual as the blurb purposely failed to provide her with the information she was looking for. However, it was now 8:30am, get reading, she thought, as she wanted to spend a good amount of time in 'Fantasy'.

Turning the thin, fragile page of paper, so easy to rip, she placed her glasses on the very edge of her nose to prepare her reading stance. The page contained a question in big bold writing.

"ARE YOU READY?"

Paying no mind, she turned to the next page, reading

"THERE'S NO TURNING BACK FROM THIS POINT ON, SO IF YOU ANSWERED 'YES' TO THE FIRST QUESTION, TURN TO THE NEXT PAGE."

Turning to the next page, it read,

"I SEE YOU ANSWERED YES THEN, AN EXCELLENT CHOICE; WELL I GUESS YOU'RE READY THEN."

Jane had become impatient with the books silly antics by now.

Turning to the next page, it read:

"ON YOUR MARKS"

...then the next page

"GET READY"

...then the next page

"GET SET"

…then finally…

"GO!"

Nothing happened. What on Earth? Jane flicked through the rest of the book frustratingly, only to find blank, plain pages full of *nothing!* Was this some sort of practical joke, she couldn't help but wonder. Going back to the page that read **GO!**' she repeated it aloud in a confused tone, **"GO!"** she uttered.

"AAAAAHHHHHHH!!!" The journey had begun.

She was blinded by the brightness; blinking her eyes harshly, she patted what felt like cushiony floor in search for her dependable glasses that had fallen off her nose. Pausing for a moment, she sensed some sort of movement or footsteps coming from her left. In her hazy vision, a short, stubby figure appeared holding her glasses out for her to take hold of; she took them gratefully. Finally, blowing on them and wiping the frames clean with her school jumper sleeve, she placed them back onto the place where they belonged. Looking up, she jerked back at the sight of seeing the most phenomenal looking thing she had ever seen in her life.

It was completely furry from head to toe, like a big teddy-bear, all cuddly and cute; it had two fluffy legs, arms and eyes with purple long lashes. It basically had similar features that a human-being contained. However, strangely it had no nose or ears.

"Me, Tippy-toe-toe!" the thing exclaimed with a squeaky high-sounding pitch.

Jane jumped back in a fright, staring intensely at this weird looking, strange speaking... *thing.*

"ME, TIPPY-TOE-TOE! ME, TIPPY-TOE-TOE! ME, TIPPY-TOE-TOE!"

Why was this thing shouting so **loud?** Jane had heard it the first time, maybe it was repeating itself until Jane revealed her identity and told it what her name was.

"My name, I mean me, Jane Pip," she said, looking at it awkwardly with her head stretched back as if in resistance to get too close.

"You, Jane Pip, You, Jane Pippy-pip, You, Jane Pippy – pip-pip."

"No, Jane Pip is just fine thank you."

"NO! YOU JANE PIPPY-PIP-PIP! YOU JANE PIPPY-PIP-PIP! YOU JANE PIPPY-PIP-PIP!"

"Alright, alright, me Jane Pippy-pip-pip."

How in the world did I get here? And what am I doing? Jane wondered. Suddenly a light bulb appeared in her head, *The Book!* But how? With no more time to ponder to herself, she suddenly sunk through her unsupportive, cushiony rest position to find herself surrounded by more extraordinary creatures that looked similar to the appearance of Tippy-toe-toe. They all spoke at once, rudely over one another, eager to introduce themselves to Jane. Jane's heart started to beat very fast; she wasn't used to so many loud voices and seeing strange looking creatures at once, after all, she is not the sociable type, *remember?*

"Tippy-toe-toe, could you tell me where I am please?"

"Aww, Jane-Pippy-pip-pip, don't'ter worry'er you'er ar'er in'er 'Fiantasy Land'er!"

In an English translation, Tippy-toe-toe had just told Jane that she was in 'Fantasy Land'.

"I'm in WHAT?!" So it was true all along! It does exist! I wonder if this is where aliens come from, the Yeti, the Loch Ness Monster and all the other so-called mythical made-up creatures!

Tippy-toe-toe offered Jane a furry arm and helped her to her feet; she struggled to stand straight as the surface she stood on seemed to be moving. Looking beneath her, she saw that she was no longer on the ground but floating in mid-fantasy air on top of a gigantic daisy. She couldn't believe her eyes; she never knew it was even possible for a flower to be so big; this was clearly unrealistic, she presumed. She dared not even look down, for she had a great phobia of heights and from what she could feel and see she was evidently high up. After a brief journey, she landed safely. Tippy-toe-toe zealously ushered her to go before him off the gigantic daisy. To keep him happy, she did as she was told. A sign hovered luminously ahead of them, with glowing lights that twinkled around it. It read 'THE FANTASY LAND TOUR ENTRANCE'. She stood dazed at how magnificently beautiful the sign was.

"Come on'er, come on'er, Jane Pippy-pip-pip!" Honestly, Tippy-toe-toe was incredibly eager for Jane to explore his homeland. Willingly she complied, and walked beyond the entrance sign into the 'Fantasy Land' tour.

One word: **WOW!** It was absolutely amazing. Indescribable. Unimaginably out of this world. You would have to see it, to believe it. Jane Pip had seen it all with her two brown eyes. She was living, seeing and breathing 'Fantasy'. It was as real as can be. The land was filled with chirpy sunshine in every visible sight she turned to look at. The land was filled with abnormal creatures of different shapes, colours and sizes; although it was hypothetically freaky, Jane was fascinated. The fantasy mid-air skies were filled with red yellow clouds, pink-orange clouds, and green-white clouds, just floating out of any and everywhere. The most peculiar thing about them was these weren't just any ordinary colourful clouds, they were edible candyfloss clouds.

"Here'er you'er can'er eats it!" Tippy-toe-toe kindly handed Jane a chunk of candyfloss cloud. And this wasn't just any candyfloss; it was pink–orange candyfloss. It was the key to her heart, after reading of course. She ate it, wasting not a mouthful, licking her fingers repeatedly; she savoured the sweet aromatic taste that lingered on her taste buds.

"More floss-floss!" insisted Tippy-toe-toe.

Jane nodded assuredly, along came the gigantic daisy again.

"Now'er we'er move'er on'er, come'er, come'er Jane Pippy-pip-pip."

Suddenly there was a change in atmosphere. The scenery was immediately ravishing pink, with a hint of strawberry flavouring. The daisy landed for Jane and Tippy-toe-toe to get off. Jane's eyes widened as she was surrounded by mammoth, scrumptious sweets! Bonbons, Opal Fruits, Skittles, Refreshers, Wham bars, Fruity Pops, Sherbet, Drumsticks, Mojos, Chewits, Love Hearts, Swizzles, Parma Violets, Ginormous of the Ginormas, Bassetts Liquorice Allsorts, and it didn't stop there: that's all her eyes were able to see.

"WEE! WEE! WEE!" Tippy-toe-toe was having a blast, as he slid laughing hysterically at the top of his furry little lungs down a chocolate-fall into a swimming pool full of it. Jane was astonishingly mesmerised at the large chocolate fountain fall, and even more delighted to see the pool of it beneath her. She was soon to follow Tippy-toe-toe's lead, by diving down the fountain fall into the chocolate pool of blissful ecstasy. That was funny, she'd lost sight of Tippy-toe-toe, and suddenly the heavy weight of a bonbon sweet ball smacked her headfirst, dazing her for a moment. It was Tippy-toe-toe clowning around.

"OI! YOU CHEEKY FUR BALL!"

She then threw it back at him, missing terribly, and so on the game continued back and forth, back and forth until the heavy bonbon sunk miserably underneath the chocolate pool.

"OH NO! bonbon gone'er, it gone'er!" Tippy-toe-toe wanted to carry on playing and was resistant to accepting the fact that it was now over. Jane trod through the thick contents of milk chocolate to get to where Tippy-toe-toe was. She comforted him is his time of disappointment. He buried his head in her body, whimpering softly into the cotton fabric of her uniform.

"There there, Tippy," patting his furry body, she saw that the gigantic daisy had arrived to take them to another part of the tour. She carried, and I mean literally, had to carry Tippy-toe-toe onto the daisy as he refused to walk. In the next breath Tippy-toe-toe was back to his normal self; well his behaviour wasn't exactly what humans would call normal. However, he was back to the 'normal' Tippy-toe-toe, doing what he did best, being loud, hyperactive and overexcited. Jane preferred him much more like this.

The gigantic daisy dropped them off onto the most ravishing green scenery, filled with a whole plant and animal kingdom. These weren't just any ordinary plants and animals, these were the plants and animals of 'Fantasy'. They were the most ludicrous looking sights she had ever come across: there were tigers with pig-feet, birds with long, floppy rabbit ears, fish with frog legs, horses with fins, monkeys with hair, oh no! Wait a minute, that was normal, but the list goes on. Here comes the most exciting part, these animals and plants could TALK! It was ridiculously insane, talking animals slightly understandable, but a plant? That's something no human in their right minds could come to terms with, it, was just UNREAL!

Yet again, Jane was fascinated. She began making conversation with a purple tulip who was a... you'd never believe it, beauty vlogger! It gave her make up tips on how to do the natural makeup look. It also advised her that she didn't need make up to feel good about herself and that true beauty came from within. The pig-footed tiger gave her tips on how to be an unbeatable gamer, she was quite intrigued and keen to try, as she always assumed that gaming was only for boys... Or at least that's what her brothers said whenever she had tried to join in with them. Tippy-toe-toe chased the floppy-eared birds around the luscious grass, repeatedly scaring them so that they couldn't settle. To him it was just a game; I couldn't say that they were in the slightest amused by his tormenting behaviour. Jane called him as a distraction from the birds, Tippy-toe-toe then began chasing her. Round and round in circles until he exhausted himself. What a character? He was amazing. The gigantic daisy had arrived in no time again, it was very efficient and always on time.

The last part of the tour, the best part of the tour, fairy tales 'gone wrong.' Jane met almost every fantasy character she had read about or watched as a child... But re-versioned. She saw the three little wolfs and the big bad pig. They invited her for a cup of tea but could only provide cold water with it and no milk as the pig had blown all the houses down. She then met Cinde-runner who had re-vamped her ball gown into a tracksuit so she could practice the 100m sprint for the next athletic championships. She also met Snow Black and the seven Rastas who taught her how to dance 'Jamaican' style. Jane was wiggling her plump body until her glasses fell off, and as for Tippy-toe-toe, he was on his head doing the splits by the end of it. I suppose that's what reggae music does to you inside. Exhausted by all the fun, Jane and Tippy-toe-toe rested at a sleepover they were invited to for the night with Sleeping Beauty, who didn't sleep at all! In fact, she was so energetic, she could have given Tippy-toe-toe a run for his money. Just when Jane and Tippy thought they were going to get some rest, Sleeping Beauty threw another party to remember, with dance challenges, games, rap battles, pizza and more!

The next morning, the gigantic daisy arrived for the final time. It dropped Jane and Tippy-toe-toe back to the entrance of the 'Fantasy Land' tour. Jane was surprised at how quickly it was all over, the creatures presented her with 'Fantasy Land' gifts of pink-orange candyfloss, a pig-footed tiger, and pictures of the characters in 'Fairy tales gone wrong'. Jane grew emotional; the journey had been so adventurous and exciting. It brought a new light to her life that she had been waiting for and she wasn't ready for its spark to die. Poor Jane Pip. Tippy-toe-toe threw his furry arms around her neck choking the dear life out of her without realising.

"TIPPY! I CAN'T BREATHE!" she squeaked.

"Oh Jane Pippy-pip-pip you'er leave'er now'er," he bawled dramatically.

Jane once again comforted Tippy-toe-toe in his time of despair and once again, he buried his furry body into the cotton fabric of her uniform. At least this time she didn't have to carry him anywhere, thank goodness for that. Within the next two breaths, Tippy-toe-toe bounced back to his normal self once again. She was used to his odd behaviour by now; as she walked towards the exit sign, she took one last look at the wonderful land of 'Fantasy' that she had experienced. Suddenly, Tippy-toe-toe came leaping towards her in a boisterous manner.

He placed a necklace round her neck gently, shaped in the form of a heart-star-moon. It read, 'Jane Pip came to Fantasy Land'. With a huge grin, she honoured the gift she was given and with that threw her arms around Tippy-toe-toe's furry neck. She held him tight not wanting to let go. He managed to wriggle free eventually, after tugging actively on her frizzy hair. As she finally walked towards the exit sign once more, she turned and waved goodbye. She then exited; the exit was more exciting than the entrance. It was a massive wet slide leading to a humungous fuchsia bouncy castle, which bounced her straight back down to Earth. Back to reality.

Colour me in

TRAPPED

Day 1 - LEFT BEHIND

THUD! It came bursting in as if it were in the 'Invincible Navy of the Spanish Armada' under the overall command of the 'Duke of Medina Sidonia 1588'. I hid behind my bedroom door quietly, not uttering a word, neither a sound. I waited anxiously for its presence to stand before my eyes. The noisesome racket it made was like the sharp rifling pain of a stab wound to my ear. SMAAAAASSH! It showed no mercy. It charged the stairs, making an awful ear-splitting sound. I managed to catch this thing glimpsing left, then right, then straight ahead: straight at me.

Stepping back with a hesitant reaction, I thought it had seen me through the crack of the door. But no, it looked away and headed straight for somebody else's room. A rush of adrenalin accelerated, like a vast blow of blazing fire in a burning bush at an expeditious pace, through my abdomen. I heaved with the nauseous fear that had unleashed its presence throughout me. I watched in horror as the creature had once again forced its way through another area of my world without invitation. This time it was another room. It was Rosie's turn. She screamed out a tremendous cry of apprehension as she was dragged carelessly out of her bedroom. I watched the abhorrent scene from behind a crack in the door.

"LET ME GO! LET ME GO!" she shrieked. These words penetrated through my mind as floods of silent tears rapidly swam down my terror-stricken cheeks. I was a coward for not even venturing to help my sister, and I knew it. How could I have stood there and watched it all happen? My hands were clasped firmly over my ears to block out the heart wrenching sounds that she made. My eyes pointed above towards the heavens, as if begging for mercy upon her soul. I wanted it to stop. I just wanted it all to stop.

After a substantial amount of time, it all too suddenly was quiet. Too quiet. I couldn't hear Rosie anymore, or the ponderous, heavy footsteps of the mysterious creature. They had gone. Rosie had been stolen from me. She was the only thing I had left, she promised that we were in this together and that this creature would not be able to take on both of us when it returned. I hate promises, Rosie. I needed her; I was defenceless without her. Collapsing slowly back against the wall, onto the bedroom floor, I was unable to function properly; I tried to make some sense of this situation. First Dad, then Mom, then Rosie, then…OH NO! NO! Yes, I had to face reality somehow; it was my turn next. The creature would be coming for me!

Day 2 – INDEPENDENCE

Awoken by the sounds of violent winds smacking the faces of my double glazed windows, it was then that my lonely world began.

The house remained dead and silent, making me feel incredibly uncomfortable. The awkwardness of no house atmosphere was actually quite alarming, as the only person who could create it was me. Everywhere I looked was a complete mess, the remains of what that creature had caused. Mom, who always liked a perfectly clean house wouldn't have stood for this. Not a chance. I tried to make the place look a bit neater, but then stopping myself, I had realised that there was no point in doing this, as the creature would be returning very soon. It was no use pretending that I could magic my life back to normal, and trying to think positively only made me feel weak.

Boredom had, without a doubt, filtered through my mind. Bedraggled by every rubbish show, game and vlog on my tablet, I gave up trying to entertain myself any longer. I was starving, but I couldn't cook, I always depended on somebody else to do everything for me. Independence was draining, like CHEAP LABOUR! I was forced to do, think and provide for myself.

10 minutes later...

I gave my attention to a pile of old books that were not even remotely interesting, none of them engaging not even a quarter of my undivided attention. It was soo sad.

5 minutes later ...

Well, look on the bright side, I HAVE A
FREE HOUSE FOR THE REST OF MY LIFE!
No, that wasn't fun. It was soo sad.
I was soo BORED! Seriously. I couldn't find anything to do. I practically had no life now. Seriously, it was soo sad!

FINALLY!

I had found a constructive way to waste my time successfully. MUSIC!
I was going to blast music ☺

10 minutes later...

Bored again.
It was no fun singing by myself. It was usually me and Rosie singing silly songs out of tune and out of time at the very top of our lungs.

0 seconds later ...

The tears had started.

0 seconds later ...

And they kept on coming.

0 seconds later ...

I just couldn't stop!

Who was I kidding, the idea of me trying to be independent was just as stupid as the idea of a dog trying to ride a bike.

Day 3 – GOING 'MAD'

ENOUGH! IS ENOUGH! IS ENOUGH!

She scowled at me aggressively so I scowled back, with teeth displayed sharp as razors! I was completely astonished at the abnormality of my appearance. I did look an awful sight. So awful, I almost scared myself. My white cotton tank top was deeply stained by the orange, mixed with yellow, contents of my own vomit. My stuffy nose was covered in nothing but mucus and the smell of dried spit from another sleepless night full of pain and sorrow. I was alone. Too alone. I was going mad in this place.

I hadn't eaten properly in the last 48 hours apart from five full glasses of concentrated 'Smart Price' apple juice. I could see that I had lost ridiculous amounts of weight as I gazed at the blurred readings on the stainless steel scales that I stood on. I threw it, like a wild-child on the loose; into the glass mirror in my bedroom. The glass shattered from the rage of my actions, making a loud, cracking exit to its death. I wanted to throw something else. It felt good. I went on throwing: books, papers, old toys, boxes; any object that made a good smashing sound when it landed.

"ARRRRRGHH, and they said that vengeance will be MINE!" I snarled at my reflection in the murdered mirror pieces, whilst showcasing my teeth angrily like a wolf venturing for its innocent prey. I looked so vicious; I looked inhuman. Hyperventilating, I sat down on the cold, smooth floor. It made me slide repeatedly as I wasn't able to catch grip with it properly.

"ARGGGGHHHH!! What the heck is wrong with me? I can't take this anymore! DAD! MOM! ROSIE! ANYBOODYY!!"

The exasperating feeling that had taken hold over me was not about to win this battle. I had to keep it together; it was not the time for my inconvenient shenanigans. But no, why shouldn't I be angry? I've had to experience the burning fumes of serious hell these last three days! Why shouldn't I be allowed to be angry? Why can't I express the hurt of losing my immediate family? The people I counted on most to keep me safe from any form of harm or danger. Why should I contain myself? WHY?

I was going mad!

I needed help.

Somebody ... Anybody ... Please ...

I was going mad in this place!

Day 4 – A SENSE OF PEACE

I was awakened by the sounds of birds singing in harmonious symphony that managed to swim lightly through the sun-rayed faces of my windows. It was then that I had felt a sense of peace. I managed to grace the broken mirror with a smug smile, with half risen cheeks. Washed clean, and dressed in fresh, soap powdered smelling fabrics, I could say I started to behave like a *normal* person again.

I treated myself to the scrumptious meal of a full English breakfast including all the trimmings. (I know, I actually *tried* to cook something!). Then to wash it all down I had a refreshing, healthy glass of tap water.

Sitting in the garden for an hour and a half; I was in deep reflection with myself. It was rather interesting, although it does sound a tad mad. I found that being still and silent helped me to get in touch with my inner self. You should try it.

I began to reflect on the importance of family and friends; it's true what they say, 'You never realise how much you truly love someone until they are gone.' You want to know the really sad thing? I never had the opportunity to tell my family and friends how much I truly loved them before they were stolen from me. I suppose you strut around thinking that nothing bad will ever happen to anyone close to you. I suppose I always thought that I was exempt. Hmm, strange that.

My Dad would always say to me *"Cheer up love, the sunshine won't stand still for you!"*

Whenever I felt myself going through this 'head thing', Mom would always hug me close and I could hear her heart racing fast, fast, FAST. One of the nights when I couldn't stop crying, and I felt like I couldn't breathe, and everything felt so small and tight around me, Mom stayed up with me all night until I cried myself to sleep. As soon as she thought I was fast asleep she would creep out, I'd then jump out of bed again and peak through the crack in my door. That's when I saw it. I saw Mom in pain. Sitting at the top of the landing, she would cry her eyes out in silence whispering something to Dad about 'mental health'. I googled it once, and found something about feeling sad and anxious.

I asked Rosie if her head ever felt really sad, but she always laughed and said *"Being sad is really boring... So it's better to keep your head happy."*

I guess she was right, being sad was boring, but sometimes I really can't help it.

3, 2, 1...

The tears have started again.

And they kept on coming again.

I just couldn't stop again!

Day 5 - STILL WAITING...

The night was young and dominating. It had been approximately two weeks, six hours and 11 seconds since this still remaining anonymous creature had been out on the loose. It had captured most of the neighbours on my road. Many that I didn't know, and many that I did. Family, friends, the postwoman called Nina. Why? It was the question that still remained. I knew that I was bound to be next. It was coming for me, and there was nothing I could do. If I ran, it would only follow. If I hid, it would only find me.

I began packing away my most sacred possessions. Just in case. In case of my 'no return', then they would be hidden, safe from eyes and hands that would never be able to have the satisfaction of claiming them. It was a sad moment.

Please brain...*No more tears.*

There was only one thing that was worse than danger itself, and that was waiting for it. It was too much to bear, still waiting. I scanned each area and every room of the house repeatedly, cherishing every single born memory that had ever once lived, happy, sad, and angry. It was a sad moment. I went into every single room, but one. Rosie's room. I couldn't. I just couldn't bring myself to go in. I just couldn't do it. Intermittently, I would start to turn the door handle, but then stopped sharply. But why was it so hard for me just to open the door and let myself in? It wasn't like the usual routine where I had to knock, because Rosie was so prestigious and personal about people just barging into her room.

Awkward Silence...

I now knew the shameful truth as to why I couldn't bring myself to go in there. I knew why, I'll even tell you why. It's because of guilt. I felt guilty for letting my sister down. I looked her directly in the face as she was being taken, the horror in her eyes, the tears of anguish and pain short lastingly living on her cheeks a moment, to then dying on her lips. I watched in horror, whilst protecting my own self. As long as I was safe, Rosie didn't matter. Shame on me.

What would you have done if you had been in my position?

I finally let myself in; the floorboards murmured as if in mourning for their owner. The room was cold and lifeless. Something didn't feel right. I had been in Rosie's room many times, however I had never felt its atmosphere the way I did now. Its preternatural sense suffocated me until I felt breathless. Trying to foster ignorance to the abnormality of what was happening to me, I stumbled over to the edge of Rosie's bed. Stroking the quilt cover softly, my hands sank deeply into the smooth enamelled fabric that was overlaid with the beautiful decorative covering of lilac butterflies. Observing the room with great speculation, I came across an unusual pile of what looked like photos. Picking them up, I began flicking through them. To my surprise I had found undiscovered family pictures. I had never seen any of them before; I actually looked nice in the majority of them for a change, too. Well, considering the fact that in most of the images in my baby albums I'm either pulling silly faces, or not looking at the camera; I was never really a photogenic child.

My eyes had immediately frozen still as I came across a picture of Rosie and me. We were both wearing matching outfits: yellow dungarees, white frilly tops, patterned with daises, and silver jelly sandals. My face lit up at how completely ridiculous we both looked, but then I began to look beyond the clothes and the silly pigtails and I saw a memory. A memory of happiness with *my sister: my Rosie.*

It was another sad moment. Leaving Rosie's room, I took one last look at it, as I knew I wouldn't be entering it again for the time being. *"I'm so sorry Rosie,"* I whispered. *"I'm so sorry".*

Returning to my room, I placed the family photos safely into the box where I had carefully laid the rest of my sacred possessions. I placed the picture of Rosie and me on top; taking one more moment to look at it, I then placed the cover over the box, shutting it tightly.

It was a sad moment.

Still waiting...

Day 6 – IT WAS TIME!

It was time. I felt it in the depths of my petrified soul. I felt the blood circulating around my heart at lightning speed. It was time. No more waiting. No more. It was time. I closed my eyes whilst in deep thought, thinking of all the bad things I had done throughout my life. But nothing, nothing I had done was so extreme for me to deserve such cruel and heartless punishment. But it was time. At approximately 23:00 hours, I remained silent, still waiting.

ASLEEP!

BANG!

What was that?

BANG!

It was time.

BANG!

The door swung open with such mighty force that everything that once stood in place in the room was now scattered on the ground. And there it stood. The figure. The anonymous thing!

I screamed, kicked and tried with great abundance in order to struggle away from its grip. It was firm and tight, leaving me no choice but to accept the situation for what it was. I felt emasculated: despite all the strength in my bones, I was just an obsolete human being.

In the open, broad nightlight of the stars, I felt the bitter wind as it smacked past my face. *The thing* opened the doors of its white vehicle, which looked like a small death trap, from what I could see. It flung me to the back seat carelessly, slamming the door with such aggression that I felt the vibrations through my chest. The seats were damp, giving off a foul smell that twisted my stomach into tiny, painful knots. *Where was this thing taking me? What was it going to do with me? I wondered what it had done with Mom, Dad and Rosie. All the neighbours, and the postwoman called Nina.*

The thing then entered the car like a thief in the night; it started up the car immediately without even once glancing back at me. It drove at a reckless speed, jilting me in the seat here, there and everywhere.

Still driving...

I felt a nervous wreck as I clamped my incisors firmly into my lips; I had never felt so close to... was this thing going to kill me? The tension was killing me enough. I just wished that everything could go back to normal, my home, my family, my life. What was happening to it? Why was this happening to it? It just didn't make any sense. Why now? I just had no answers; left clueless and confused, there was just no justice.

The car had finally stopped; we, well it and me, had arrived at its destination safely. Out of the white van got the reckless driver – the thing. *SILENCE.* Wham! The door was swung open, the breeze that rushed in with it was bitter and thick.

The thing stood and looked straight through me with its agonizing stare. It then grabbed me by the ankles, hurling me in the most aggressive manner onto the hinge point of its broad shoulder blade. It was just a matter of time before my eyes were exposed to complete darkness. Unable to see, unable to feel, unable to touch, unable to hear a sound of my world.

Day 7 – TRAPPED

'Dear Lord', I cried inside my head...
If there was ever a time for me to believe in your existence, it would be now.
Nan always said we must say our prayers before tea and bedtime, but I'm going to pretend that it's tea time now.
Please forgive me for all the bad things I have ever done throughout my life.

I'm even sorry for the time I called Charlie stupid, for the time I ate that last bit of Dad's birthday cake and lied about eating it, the time I didn't brush my teeth before bed and the time... the time, *I left Rosie.*

I just pray, I pray that you keep me alive.

I also pray that it hasn't hurt any of my family or friends.

Amen.

After praying for the first time in ages, I felt secure and at peace, as if I had been really heard.

There was an interminable mood that seized the dishevelled surroundings. It was seemingly long and endless. The foreboding darkness abruptly sucked up every sumptuous thing in sight, like a malevolent vacuum cleaner, leaving nothing incongruous; leaving nothing untidy. It felt like I had been here for a lifetime. I sat waiting. Waiting in this unfamiliar, dismayed place; however, I tried hard to control the sad part of my brain, I tried hard not to feel really sad, and I tried really, really, really hard not to cry. But not knowing where I was or what was going to happen next was *scaarry.*

My environment felt haughty and violent, with a horrendous stench that was hard to breathe in.

What kind of mad thing would live here?

A lustrous glimpse of foreign moonlight managed to glisten softly through a dainty crack in the wall. The alertness of its gaze distinctively focused on my face, like yellow sunrays burning through a piece of glass. It made me feel a sense of relief and peace, just like on 'Day 4'. To me this light was significant as it represented the light at the end of my dark tunnel.

The supercilious gaze of this daunting, obscure creature had taken its hold over me, sustaining utter focus, as if in refusal to restrict its attention from my sight. I couldn't see it, but I felt the burning duplicity of its aura, as it's sinister, savaged pupils penetrated mine. My palms were sweaty, I wrung my hands, and my heart was beating, fast, fast, FAST. I knew I was in danger: alone and afraid. My body sat, terribly uncomfortable in its position, as uninviting blows of constant chills submerged my pale skin with electrical impulses of consistent shivers. Backwards, then forwards, I rocked hesitantly as if trying to bring myself to some sense of reality.

Bah, bum, THUD! bah, bum, were the sounds of my heart as it pounded against the surface of my chest, in the prospect of blood-curdling terror.

I did everything in my willpower to defeat this overwhelming feeling. I even began to reminisce about the freedom I once had, before being captured into this traumatic, doom hole. I began to remember, distinctively, the days I sat waiting for this day to finally come to pass, and here it was. I hated it with a vengeance! I wish I had never been born to see this day. I just wanted to forget it all. Forget that I was even here, experiencing such horror. I wanted to block out the negative energy that violated and suffocated me slowly.

I began to imagine the vivid imagery of a luxurious breeze appearing in the centre of my thoughts. It then swam gently through the air holes of my small, buttoned nose, whilst echoes of birds singing sweetly filled the drumming in my ears. I saw a ravishing plantation swaying in a sensational motion as if dancing in rhythmic pace to its atmosphere, whilst Mom, Dad, Rosie and I sat in a circle laughing harmoniously with one another. It was just like I had remembered. It was exquisitely, delightfully… just a dream!

I regretfully re-opened my eyelids to revisit the grotesque appearance of my surroundings. My ears were then alerted to the disturbing sounds of heavy breathing. Even more disturbingly, there was not a sound being made by the thing! Panic-stricken, I bit my lips intensely as this strange sound appeared to be growing even louder. Looking in every possible direction, I was determined to distinguish where this sound was coming from. It had entwined itself with the open air, creating a belligerent presence that vibrated vigorously against my body.

As it did this, the thing continued to unlock its glaring eyes from my sight. Its gaze grew more commanding along with the brutal sound. This made me emphatically vulnerable. I saw no way out. I was now at my wit's end and needed to be freed.

I was trapped.

As I opened my eyes, Dad, Mom, Rosie and Nan all surrounded the bed.
Then Nan started to pray...
"Dear God,
We thank you for Tilly.

We thank you that she is here in a safe place where she can get better. I pray your angels stay by her side at this most difficult time of her life and that the staff here can do everything in their power to give her the help and support she needs.
Amen"
"*Amen."* Everyone echoes.
"Mom?"
"Yes sweetie"

Oh no… I can feel the tears coming again.

"The thing… The thing inside my head… It makes me feel very sad. I feel trapped. I can't stop crying."

"Don't worry sweetheart," Dad says as he takes my hand. "You're going to get all the help you need."

Acknowledgements

People I need to thank:

God: **For blessing me with the wonderful gift of making stuff up that people actually find entertaining and want to read.**

My Year 9 English Teacher: **Mrs Ferreira, thank you for refusing to accept my second best.**

My amazing parents: **Dennis and Esha Johnson who have always told me 'I can'.**

My sister: **Delena Johnson who helps me A LOT behind the scenes (you're truly awesome!!)**

My sister: **Shara Johnson who has always encouraged me to believe that I'm FABULOUS just the way I am.**

And, thank you to:

My family and friends who support and encourage me in all of my ambitious and (sometimes) crazy ideas, thank you for standing in my corner, cheerleading me from the sideline and just being YOU!

And thank you to YOU, the reader, for picking this book. Enjoy, and remember to colour in the pictures!

Glossary

A Dupey - A ghost

Badda - Bother

Caan/Cyaan - Can/Can't

Dis - This

Dutty Wine - A West Indian dance

Er - Her

Farse - Saying or doing something
you have no business in

Fi - To

Fi yuh - For you

Gwarn - Go

Ha fi - Have/had to

Im - Him

Ital Herbs - Vegetation

Jam - Song

Luk - Look

Mek - Make

Mi - Me

Pickney - Child

Sei - See

Sekkle - Settle

Shelly Belly - A dance, named after a Jamaican
dancer 'Shelly Belly'.

Shud - Should

Tank yuh - Thank you

Tek - Take

The Bogle - A dance, named after Jamaican
dancehall star 'Mr. Bogle'

The Butterfly - A Jamaican dance move

Tings - Things

Trow - Throw

Tu - To

Waan - Want

Wah - What

Wei yard - Our house

Whey mi deh? - Where am I?

Whu - Who

Widout - Without

Wud - Would

Yu - You